CECIL LONGSTREET

THE BEGINNING

BY

MARVIN B. BLATT

America Star Books

Softcover 9781611027174
PUBLISHED BY AMERICA STAR BOOKS, LLLP
www.americastarbooks.com

Printed in the United States of America

ACKNOWLEDGEMENTS:

To my dear Shelly,

To my son Marc and his wife Rachel,

I love you all.

CHAPTER 1

Once upon a time, in a small town north of London, England, lived a boy named Cecil, that's me...Cecil Longstreet is my name. I was born on October 13, 1947, into a magical, yet mysterious family. Well, that's what the people on the south side of town are saying.

I live in the north side of a town called Stoneway. It has a population of about 400 people. One hundred of them live in the north and I know all of them. My family has lived in this area for over 300 years, so my family is well known by all who live here. I know every inch of this town.

The two sections of Stoneway are separated from one another only by a lake. This lake is only 20 feet wide at its widest, and 10 feet wide the more you travel towards the eastern part of the town. The people on the south side of the lake call the north side, where I live, the strange part of town.

Well, I suppose that the people from the south side are right. They do have a point. I mean, you can't blame them for thinking the way they do. There's no hiding the fact that we have witches, a wizard and all sorts of people who perform all sorts of magic, all living in my area, the north side of town.

Now, don't get me wrong, the people on the south side are not bad people. There was a time when we all lived in peace and harmony, but that was centuries ago, way before I was born, that's for sure. I'll tell you more about that later. I don't want to get ahead of myself.

Up until I was ten years old, I wasn't allowed to cross the lake alone. For the first ten years of my life, I really had no reason to cross that lake anyway. We had our stores and we even had our own school. The people who live on the south side had their own stores and their own school as well. Our school was used by the families with special talents. That would be every family in the north. Using the term "special talents" was a nice way of indicating to anyone in the south that we in the north have special powers. And again, they're right, we do have special powers.

In my school, we were taught the ways of the people in the south and the culture of my people. The school in the south didn't believe in what my people did, nor did they understand my people, so they didn't attempt to teach what they knew nothing about. In my school, we taught both cultures. We were told that we were getting a well-rounded education by doing that. Besides, it's always good to know the ways of your neighbors. I crossed the lake to visit my friends.

You're probably wondering how I met these friends, especially if I wasn't allowed on the other side of the lake. That's very simple. Well, both the north side and south side children shared the lake and loved to swim in it. Not all of the south side kids were allowed to associate with us. Only a few dared try. And the same can be said for the north side kids. The relations between the two territories are getting a little bit better, but it's going to take a very long time for everyone to come around. There were children who were not allowed to even come close to us. The parents were afraid that we would turn their kids into fish, or something like that. The parents were afraid of the special talented kids. Some parents downright despise us so much that they still call us young witches, or witches in training. Neither of these statements would hurt my feelings. My friends, after getting to know me, know and understand that I am not going to hurt them. You see, I am not a witch yet, so I have no powers. My friends know that. We actually have a lot in common. I said that I have friends that I talk to. That doesn't mean that their parents approve or even know of our friendships. Come to think of it, none of the parents know that we even talk to each other. That would include my parents as well. You see, my parents are very old fashioned. If they knew that I was talking to those people in the south, well let's just say, who would want to be turned into a toad? I'm only kidding. They would turn me into a rabbit.

I haven't quite figured it out, but something happened centuries ago, and it looks like nobody will ever forgive and forget. When I said relations between the two territories is getting better, that is the truth. The people in the south side are not throwing rocks at us anymore. Every so often, some even wave from across the lake, half-heartedly, along with a fake smile. I understand that the rock throwing stopped about 100 years ago. Nobody forgives or gives an inch around here… on both sides. I really do hope that everyone will live in peace someday.

Besides using a rowboat to get to the other side, there is a bridge, a very old bridge that gets you over the lake and into the south side of Stoneway. This bridge is so old; it is made up of rope and wooden planks. On a windy day, the bridge will swing sideways. You have to be careful, or you will wind up in the lake. I meet my friends on the bridge during the week. This way, neither one of us is in each other's territory. It's a neutral meeting place. Since we cannot call each other on the telephone, one of us must walk onto the bridge and hope that the other can see him or her standing on the bridge. I don't know what we would do if that bridge gives way. Who would fix it? I know my parents wouldn't fix it. All I know is, it would be the end of my seeing my friends, I'm afraid, for a very long time.

There is something else that bothers the people in the south side of town…the way we dress. We tend to dress with very bright colors. Our shirts are usually red or yellow, but a bright red and yellow. Our pants are usually yellow or orange, but a very bright yellow and orange color. We dress by the meaning of the colors we wear. Part of our lives is directed by the meaning of colors. For instance, the color yellow has several meanings. I wear yellow because it is associated with mourning. It also means happiness. It is a tribute to friends and family who have left this earth. The color red represents a soldier. I am a soldier for my cause. What cause? To someday make people believe and understand that what my people do with their magic is real, not an illusion; it's real. The color orange is associated with joy and sunshine. So as you can see, everything, even what we wear, has a meaning and fulfills a purpose. The tradition of putting a meaning to color is part of my culture, which goes back to the very beginning of my people.

Before I forget, I just remembered one more thing. Besides throwing rocks at us, something much more serious has never been forgotten by my people. Approximately 300 years ago, witches were being hung down by the lake, and this happened often. If a witch dared cross over to the other side, he or she always took the chance of being caught and hung. Well, this got my people up in arms, and they finally put a stop to all of this. My people, led by Winston Longstreet, stopped all of this hanging by starting to use their magic. Now we were telling them, yes, you are right, we are witches. But my people didn't care. At least it stopped all of the hangings. Both sides pulled their people back and nobody has really had a conversation with those on the other side since then. You do have those people who think that that was then, and none of us had anything to do with what happened 300 years ago...so let's talk. We have a few from both sides that think that way, but too few to convince anyone that a relationship with their neighbors will work. Not very promising. It is going to take a lot of work and changing a lot of minds of a lot of stubborn people... including my parents.

CHAPTER 2

I am what the people from the south side call me, a witch in training. Even though this magic thing is in my blood, I still have a lot to learn about it. Heck, I wouldn't know one spell from another. I have seen them performed, but have no idea how they are done. It's not like if you turn 10, you go into training. It's not that simple. It's actually up to the head of the household. In my case, it would be my father, the Head Wizard and only wizard in this part of town. My father would be the equivalent of the chief of an Indian tribe or the President of the United States. Actually, my father did come to me right after my 10th birthday and sat me down and explained to me that he wanted to talk to me, alone.

"Son, I asked for this talk for a reason. I believe that it is time for you to go into training."

"Training for what, Father?"

"It is in your eyes and a feeling that I have, that tells me that it is time for you to become a witch. And, hopefully, one day, a wizard, just like your father. And who knows, maybe you'll even become the Witch of London, just like your older cousin, Stephen."

"Okay, when do we start?"

"Tomorrow. Tomorrow morning. I want you in my study at 10 o'clock in the morning."

"Should I bring something special? Do I need to gather toads or herbs?"

"No, no, just show up. We will start from the beginning. We will begin on page one. You will learn to walk before you run."

"Father, I have been waiting for this moment my whole life!"

"Son, you are just 10 years old. Anyway, I started at 10 years old, and I believe you are ready."

"How do you know that I am ready? I mean, you look into my eyes and you can tell?"

"Am I not the mighty wizard of this territory? Wasn't your grandfather, Winston Longstreet, the one who founded this territory, and was the first wizard of this territory? Don't you think that I would know when you are ready?"

"Sorry. I guess I wasn't thinking. I now realize how stupid that question was."

"Don't ever doubt me again, Son. You must trust your wizard, for he is a wise and powerful man. And, besides, you should always listen to your father. And let's not forget…listen to your mother as well. You know that she is a powerful witch."

I entered my father's study with 15 minutes to spare. I found the largest chair in the room and got lost in it. I sat up straight and thought about what is going to happen when my father the wizard comes through that door. My father's study is a very large room. As a matter of fact, every room in this house is very large. We have the largest house in this town. The south side houses are very small houses compared to this one. I just remembered. There is another house that is larger than ours. It's the house of the Witch Of London. There are rooms in that house that can hold my whole house in it. It is what you would call a huge mansion. It is located near Stonehenge, as a matter of fact, right down the road from it. There is a reason for the Witch of London living so close to Stonehenge. One of the reasons is that the Witch of London holds the key to open the gate of Stonehenge, and another reason is that the Witch of London has work to do at Stonehenge. I don't quite understand that part, but maybe some day I will.

My house is right behind the Witch of London's house. We are separated by a few hundred acres.

Suddenly the door to the study opened and my father entered. He was dressed in a brightly colored robe and he was even wearing his pointed hat. My father is a very tall person, with extremely long hair that falls over his shoulders. His presence would make anyone get the feeling that this man is very powerful. My father demands respect and he gets it. His robe is purple for royalty and his hat is yellow. The color of the hat shows respect for our ancestors. My father's shirt is a bright green, signifying life. My father enjoys life to its fullest. His pants are orange, for joy. Why wouldn't my father be full of joy? He has everything a person could want and people respect him. Tell me that that isn't a happy man. Well, sometimes.

"Hello, Son."

"Good morning, Father."

Now is the time when you stood up to show respect.

"Sit down, my son."

So I did.

"Now that you know why you are here, let's get started."

"Father, how long will this process take? I mean, how long will it take for me to become a witch?"

"Well, you do know that just because you were born into this family, it doesn't automatically make you a witch, right?"

"Yes, I know."

"The first step is for you to want to become a witch. You must tell me that you want it. It's a title, not something that will be handed to you. Anybody could walk around and say that he or she is a witch. It doesn't mean that they really are. You will be learning about our history and, of course, magic spells. The most important thing that you will learn will be discipline. You will learn when to use your spells and you will learn when not to use them. I want you to understand that if you ever use your magic to hurt someone, your magic will be taken away from you and you will be severely punished."

"Yes, I do agree to study to become a witch. But, Father, didn't our people use magic against the people from the south a very long time ago?"

"Son, magic was used to stop them from hanging any more of us. They wanted to wipe us off of the face of the earth. There is a difference between that and just hurting someone because you don't like them. Our people used their magic to defend themselves. Please, learn the difference. It is very important for you to know that. You will be taking certain tests and you will be reading a lot of books. Since school is out now, it would be a perfect time to start. That means you will be constantly busy. Very little time for playing. There will be times when your studies are going well, and I will allow you to go out and play."

"What do you want to teach me today?"

"Today I will give you a book. Let's call it Book One. It is a very old book, and very fragile. You must be very careful with it."

Behind my father's huge desk was a bookshelf. It was built from the floor to the ceiling and from one wall to the next. The ceiling in this room is 60 feet high and the width of this particular wall is 120 feet. I'm talking about thousands of books. Well, to my surprise, a book on the top shelf was jiggling itself free from the other books. Suddenly, the book flew from above and gently landed in my lap.

"Take this book and read it every minute that you get. As you can see, it is called, Studying To Be A Witch, Book One. It was written in the 1600s."

I looked the book over for a few seconds, and then looked at the author's name.

"Father, this author has the same last name as us."

"Of course he has the same last name. He is your great, great, great, great, grandfather. Now, you may leave my study. I want to see you in three days. This book has only a 100 pages in it. It should not take you that long to read it-- and try to remember what you are reading."

"Same time as today, Father?"

"Yes."

"Father."

"Yes."

"Before I leave this room, could you please tell me how many books I have to read and how long will it be before I can become a witch?"

"I will tell you that it will take a long time. You will have to read many books. I will not give you the number of books you have to read, because I don't want that number on your mind. It will only distract you from your studying."

"That many, huh?"

"Yes."

I got up from that huge chair, carrying my first book, the one that was going to help me on my way to becoming a full-fledged witch. This made me very happy. Not only was I going to be a witch someday, I would have the attention of my father for a long time, more so than before. This made me very happy.

CHAPTER 3

My Mother

Now, let me introduce to you my mother the witch. She is what the queen is to her country. She is the Queen of Stoneway. If something drastically happens to my father the wizard, she will then take over the throne, until another wizard is chosen. There are many witches in this town that would love to become wizard. We would not have a hard time finding candidates for the position. I only hope that my father lives a very long life, and by then, I would take over the throne, only because I am his son. If I never gained the title of witch, I would not be able to become the Wizard of Stoneway. Then and only then, can someone from the outside of the family become the wizard. I already have it in my head that I am going to make a very good witch. I haven't opened my book yet and I have three days to do so, and I already know that I will make a good witch. That's confidence for you.

My mother the witch. She is a beautiful lady with long blond hair, who is very dedicated to her wizard. I never, ever, saw them argue. Never. What a relationship. I have no brothers or sisters, so I get a lot of attention from my mother. Besides being a great mother, she is also a great cook. I'll give you an example why I love to watch her cook.

First off, I stand out of the way. She then places her bowls on a counter to mix a salad or whatever she has in mind. Then she talks out loud, and spews out some words and the next thing you know, the bowls are floating above the counter. She says more words and the refrigerator door flings open. A head of lettuce comes out of the refrigerator and hangs above bowl number one. Then she'll say something else and a few tomatoes come floating out of the refrigerator, stop and hang in mid-air above bowl number two. Then my mother will outstretch her arms and say some other words, and the next thing you know, two knives are coming out of their holders from under the counters and are heading straight to bowl number one. The next thing you know, the knives are cutting up the lettuce. I mean slicing them this way and that way. As the knives are cutting up the lettuce, the lettuce is dropping into bowl number one, all chopped up. One knife then goes over to the hanging tomatoes and makes the neatest slices. The other knife heads for the sink to be washed. Watching the food drop into the bowl is something that I never get tired of seeing. What a sight to see. Now the tomatoes are sliced up and the other knife goes into the sink to be washed. Now we have two bowls hanging in mid-air. My mother says a few more words and suddenly bowl number two dumps the tomatoes into bowl number one. Get this, they are mixing themselves up! Bowl number two returns to the counter, only to wait for the next food. By the time the salad is made, the meat is cooked and brought to the table along with a loaf of bread and the drinks. Anyone would be dizzy just watching her cook. My mother is the best non- cook in this town. Don't kid yourself, very few witches really cook. Their hands very rarely touch the food. And why should they? It's not necessary and, besides, it wouldn't be as exciting to watch.

CHAPTER 4

One of the jobs that a queen has is to meet with her people if they are having problems. These meetings are held in a building on our property, not far from the main house. The only people who are allowed to attend these meetings are people who are invited to attend. If you request a meeting with the queen, it must be put into the form of a letter and then you wait for a reply from the queen. The queen will listen to your problems and then she will decide if she will handle the problem. If not, she will pass it along to the wizard. Even though my mother is a powerful person with a title, she is till the secretary to the wizard.

Now, let me tell you about what my mother usually wears: a dress that hangs to the ground, with tiny mirrors attached.

My mother's dresses are either bright red, or bright green, colors that go so well with her beautiful blond hair. As the Queen, she is always carrying around a stick about 18 inches long, with a star attached to the end of it. I've seen her use it many times when she had to perform magic. I believe it is called a wand.

Once I saw her stop a little boy from running into a tree at top speed. She froze the little boy where he stood, so he couldn't move, just as he was going to plow right into the tree. After he was stopped, she stepped between the little boy and the tree and then pointed the wand at him. The little boy then ran into the queen at full force, not the tree. The boy then got a lecture from the queen about running and not watching where he was going.

The most amazing thing that I have ever seen her do with a wand happened last summer. I was walking through the yard with my mother and she told me that she wanted to show me what she could do with the wand. We both walked over to a rose bush. A bee was flying around a rose. My mother pointed right at the bee, and froze the bee in midair. I mean, it was about an eighth of an inch away from the flower. I thought that that was the greatest thing I had ever seen. My mother then said some words, and the bee continued on its flight into the rose. I never forgot these two incidents.

Being that my father is the wizard and my mother is the queen, our family lives a very good lifestyle. We want for nothing. Another service that my family does for its people is to see that our people are taken care of. My mother will give money to the needy who live in our community. Anyone in the community that can help another needy person is supposed to outstretch their arms to help. The rule is, if you can help, do so.

Someone's roof was leaking and they met with my mother. My mother came over and gave them the money to get their roof fixed. Not long after that, people showed up to fix their roof.

My father has insisted that he didn't want the community to look like it was falling apart. He wanted everyone to be proud to live where they live. He also insisted that his part of town would always look much better than the south side. My father insists that poverty will not exist in the north.

Most important of all, my mother helps me. Besides helping me with my schoolwork, she is always there for me. I couldn't ask for anything more.

CHAPTER 5

After I woke up, I got out of bed. I then headed for the kitchen. My mother and my father were already there.

"Good morning, Son," said my mother.

"Good morning, Mother."

My father just picked up his hand and waved to me while he was reading his newspaper, The Daily Spell. So I waved back, even though I knew he didn't see me. I brought my Book One with me so that I could review some of what I read while I sat at the table. As I sat down at the table and opened my book, a bowl of cereal came out of nowhere and settled down in front of me. The milk came next and then the spoon. The milk was pouring into the bowl all by itself.

As soon as the milk stopped pouring, the spoon jumped into the cereal bowl. After watching this display of magic, and believe me, it still amazes me, I kind of figured out why I get so excited over all of this magic. I believe it's because I am not a witch yet, a boy without magical powers. I suppose once I get my powers, all of this will just be an everyday event that will no longer excite me.

"Son, you do know that today is the day that you will be tested on Book One?"

"Yes, father, I know, and I am ready."

"We'll see," said my father, from behind the newspaper.

After breakfast, I again entered my father's study and sat in my favorite over-sized chair. My father was not far behind me. When the chimes went off in the old grandfather clock, the large doors opened and my father entered the study, walking straight to his desk. He sat down and looked right at me to tell me that he wanted to get started.

"I am a very busy man." He always has something going. He is the busiest man I have ever known.

"There are questions that I have to ask you, even though you might think that they are ridiculous. Do you understand?"

"Yes."

"Did you read the book?"

"Yes, yes I did."

"I will ask you that question for every book. If you ever tell me that you did not read a book, then that session will be cancelled and you will be that far behind. Do you understand?"

"Yes."

"I can't have you or anyone else wasting my time."

"I wouldn't do that, Father."

"My first question is pretty easy. Again, did you read every single word in Book One?"

"Twice, sir."

"Let's continue. What qualities do you need to become a good witch? Think before you answer."

I thought hard, but just like in school, when I'm under pressure, I drew a blank. After calming down, the answers come to me.

"Honesty would be one."

"Good."

"Hard work."

"Which includes what?"

"Studying. A good witch never stops studying."

"That is correct. One more."

"Respect. Respect everyone in your family and community."

"Right."

"Father, is there anything that I am supposed to do in my studies concerning, let's say, the people of the south side?"

"Yes, you will always be on your guard. You never know what they will do next."

"Yes. It is going to take a lot of work."

"Another question. If someone needs our assistance, from this community, what do you do?"

"I would drop what I am doing, because what I am doing is never more important than helping someone in need."

"Right. That's all for today."

"I read this book from cover to cover for three days and these are the questions you ask me, Father?"

"I didn't say that the questions were going to be hard. The first is always the easiest. Besides, you learned a few things and that brings you a little closer to becoming a witch. Remember, I told you that you are going to walk before you run. Yes, that is all."

I looked at him and asked him what was next. He told me to keep reading that same book. I couldn't believe it. I knew that I had to listen. Ever argue with a wizard? Of course you haven't.

"So, Father, my next assignment will be to read this book again?"

"That's what I said. See you in three days, same time."

I left my father's study in a hurry and very confused. Something wasn't right. I had it in my head that I was to be going from book to book, not stay in one book after a test was given. I felt I was going in slow motion. I returned to my room and started reading my book for the fourth time. I stayed in my room for the rest of the day, just reading that book over and over again, and it seemed like I had the whole book memorized.

I had my father's permission to go into town the next day. I wanted to get a writing pad so I could do some writing on a book that I have in mind. Since I haven't learned how to fly yet, I have to walk to town. I happened to look up as I was walking and I could see amongst many flying witches, the Stewart family flying in a straight line heading towards town. Today was the day that people headed for the market for food.

I couldn't get my mind off that little speech from my father about just being kind to your own kind. It really rubbed me the wrong way. I do have friends who live in our community. I just can't believe that I have to stay away from my friends from the south side. How did my father know what I was doing to meet my friends? He knew that I was trying to meet them on the bridge. According to the book and my father, I am not supposed to ever make friends outside of our community. It's the stick to your own kind speech. I don't like it at all. Will I change my thoughts about that when I become a witch? I don't know. I might not have a choice in this matter. When I become a wizard, there might be room for change. I'll surely consider change. I believe everyone should be treated the same. I don't have to be everyone's friend, just treat everyone with respect.

As I got closer to the town, air traffic got a little busier. I could see several families flying around seeking out their favorite stores. It's the adults flying around. Their children have to walk because they are not witches yet. Some parents actually carry their children under their arms as they fly through the air and kids were actually dropped from the sky. Holding your child when you fly caused more accidents last year than anything else. My father is about to pass a law outlawing such behavior. He wants it stopped.

"Cecil!"

I heard my name called. It was Billy, a mate from school.

"Cecil, what are you doing going to town?"

"I'm taking time out of my studies. I'm going to be a witch, you know. Well, someday. It's a lot of work, Billy."

"Your father thought is was time, huh?"

"Yes."

"My father said that I am too young."

"Billy, my father told me that he began his studies at 10. He also told me that by looking into my eyes, he could tell that I am ready to begin my studies."

"Your father is the wizard, Cecil. He knows best. He is a wise man. You are a very luck boy. I was not born into royalty. I was born into poverty. That was changed a bit, when your mum came around to help us out. I have to tell you, Cecil, the word around town is that your family is running out of money…only because your family has helped so many people."

"Billy, let me put your mind and everyone else's mind at ease. We're not running out of money, far from it, so relax."

"I'm relieved to hear that. I guess if I hear a rumor, come right to the source."

"Exactly, Billy."

"The community really loves your family. We are all so very grateful to them."

"Thanks, Billy. It is our duty to help our own kind. We love doing it."

"You know, Cecil, I have figured out that this whole community is one big happy family. Even though I have a mother and a father, your parents are like parents to me as well."

"That's true, and you are like a brother to me, Billy."

"Thanks, Cecil. I feel honored."

"You're welcome."

"Why are you going to town, Cecil?"

"I'm going to the store because I want to buy a writing tablet. I was thinking about writing a book. But who knows when it will be finished. I love to write, always have."

"What kind of book? What will it be about?"

"Can't tell you now. What are you doing going to town?"

"I was following my parents into town. My neck is hurting me from constantly looking up. My parents love to fly, and I'm too heavy to carry." Billy pointed to his parents who were now on the ground.

"Well, Cecil, maybe it is a good idea to stop parents from carrying their children while they are flying. It caused too many accidents last year. My parents just landed. I'm going to catch up to them. Got to go."

As Billy got farther away from me, he turned around and yelled out. "Let's play basketball someday. Maybe even go fishing."

"That would be nice. See you later."

Later, I put my writing tablet on my desk, and then took Book Number One and walked over to my bed. I lay down and started to read my book. In a matter of a couple of minutes, I was fast asleep.

CHAPTER 6

I jumped out of bed, my shirt soaked with sweat. I ran out of my room, yelling, "Mother! Mother!"

I yelled as loud as I could, until my mother stopped me at the foot of the stairs.

"I'm here, Cecil. What's the matter? Calm down."

My mother was holding onto my shoulders and looking right into my eyes.

"Cecil, look at me and tell me what is bothering you. You are all sweaty."

"Mother, I had this dream…it was terrible!"

"Calm down. Come over to this chair and sit down."

I sat down and held my head, which was now starting to pound with pain.

"All I remember is that it was a very bad dream. Then I remembered what my father said about dreams."

"What did your father say about dreams?"

"He said the dreams that bring you to tears are dreams that will most likely come true. Mother, this dream can't come true, it just can't!"

"You still haven't told me about the dream. It can't be that bad."

"Is it true what father said? Do you believe that?"

"Yes, it is usually something that does come about. Now, again, please tell me about the dream."

So I told my mother about the dream. By the time I was finished telling her, I was still wiping my eyes and my mother's face had a look of panic.

"Cecil, for now, go back to your room, get back in bed and calm down. I will call you down for supper. In the meantime, rest on your bed. Everything will be all right. I will talk to your father. He will know what to do."

"Mother, promise me that Father will take care of this."

"I promise."

As Mother walked away, she looked very thoughtful about promising me that my father would take care of what was bothering me.

After supper, I went back to my bed. Not a word had been said during supper. I didn't awake till the next morning. When I woke up, I walked out of my room this time, holding my book. I knew that my father wanted to see me on the following day. I must have read my book eight times. I wanted to be ready for more questions.

As I entered the kitchen, I noticed a look of concern on my father's face.

"Cecil, how are you? Your mother came to me and told me the whole story."

"I'm a little bit better. I stopped crying like a baby."

"There is no crime in crying. Grown men cry. It seems to me that my boy has feelings," said my mother.

"Can we discuss my dream now?"

"Not now. Eat your breakfast," demanded my father.

This time, my bowl of food was waiting on the table for me. I thought I saw a few slightly puzzled looks passing between my parents. Maybe the wizard still didn't have an answer and neither did my mother, the queen.

"What are your plans today, Cecil?" my mother asked.

"I thought that I would sit out in the yard and read my book."

"Cecil, take the day off. Go out and play. I am sure you have read that book from cover to cover many more times since we last met."

"Yes, Father, and I am on my eighth reading."

"Go play with that nice boy, Billy. A matter of fact, why don't you invite him over to go fishing with you down by our lake?"

"I will do that, Father, thanks."

"Cecil."

"Yes, Father."

"Leave your book here."

I put his book down on the kitchen table. I turned my head and smiled at my mother and then I looked at my father and smiled at him as well. I ran down the hallway and out the front door and kept running until I got to Billy's front door. Once I arrived, I knocked on the door and Billy's mother came to the door.

"Hello, Cecil, how is everything?"

"Fine, is Billy home?"

"Yes, let me get him."

I stood on the porch thinking about what Billy's mother asked me. I knew that I wasn't all right, but I wasn't about to tell Billy's mother about my dream. It was a little white lie, but harmless. I thought that even my father would have approved of that white lie.

Every time I try to make a decision, I always ask myself, would my father approve? If the answer is yes, then I go ahead with what I am contemplating.

Billy was now standing at the door and I realized that Billy was bowing his head.

"Hi Cecil, nice to see you."

Billy has always treated me like royalty, even though technically I'm not royalty yet. When I make the grade of witch, then I would be the equivalent of a prince.

There are still people in the territory who show me respect by bowing their heads when I am close enough. I enjoy it, so I don't stop them. When I am walking with either my mother or father or both, I stand back, so that my parents can get all of the attention, the attention I believe they rightly deserve.

"Billy, how would you like to come over to my place and go fishing?"

"I'd love that. Must ask my mum."

Billy ran to the other side of his house. It didn't take him long. It is a small house. Billy came running back, this time with his fishing pole, a bucket and his lucky bobber.

"What are we waiting for?" asked Billy.

I just smiled, and we continued walking side by side down a long road. It was a beautiful day. The suns rays were coming through the trees as if the trees had holes in them. The birds were singing, the sun was out, not a cloud in the sky. A perfect day.

As we walked along, I had a hard time getting my dream out of my head. I wasn't going to share my dream with Billy. Why bring Billy down? Billy's had a very rough life, which was improved upon when my mother stepped in. Billy's family is forever grateful to the Longstreets.

We are the same age, but Billy and I are definitely opposites. I am practically royalty and Billy is very poor. Yet we have a lot in common. We both love fishing. So off we went, continuing our journey, our quest to get to our favorite place to fish.

CHAPTER 7

"Cecil, isn't it past your bedtime?" my mother asked.

"Yes, I suppose so."

I took my book from the kitchen table and headed for the walk up the long stairway. It seemed to continue up into the sky, it was that high up.

"Good night, Son," my father said.

I stopped on the first few steps and turned around.

"I'm afraid."

"Son, you know where our room is," said Father.

My mother gave me the thumbs up sign. That assured me that everything was going to be all right. I returned the thumbs up, turned around and went up the stairs to the top landing. Once at the top, I continued to the right and down the hall to the wing my bedroom occupied. On that same wing was a playroom, my own library, and a few more rooms, including three guest rooms. It could get lonely up there. But to be scared and lonely, that is a different story. Truth be told, I have a hard time being the only child up there. Sometimes I wish that my parents would give me loads of siblings--at least six brothers and maybe even a sister. I've never expressed my feelings about being the only child to my parents, though.

It took a while before I closed my eyes. I opened my book and read a few more chapters. It didn't take long for me to fall asleep once I started reading. I fell asleep with the book open and resting on my chest.

"I promised the boy that you would take care of his problem."

"You mean his dream?" asked the wizard.

"Yes."

"Even I might have a problem with this. Let me think about how I can handle this one."

"It's because you told him a while ago that if someone wakes up crying, the dream will probably come true."

"That's right," said the wizard.

"Do you think that you could be wasting time, procrastinating like this?"

"I'll get right on it."

The wizard got up and out of his chair.

"I'll be in my study."

Once inside of the study, the wizard headed for his desk. He sat down, turned around and looked at the thousands of books.

Can these books help me? I have never faced anything like this before in my whole life. The whole community will be lost. Lives will be lost. We could be wiped off the face of the planet. Now it is on my shoulders.

The wizard put his hands to his face and a small tear from his right eye quickly dropped over his right cheek. He then closed his eyes, as if to meditate.

Please, Winston, please, give me the strength that I need.

Today is the day that I would be tested on Book One. Again, I was in the study, waiting patiently for my father. From my favorite chair, I could see that my father has been busy. A bunch of books are sitting on the desk and a few are opened, as if he was working on something. Did I dare ask my father about the books?

The large door opened and Father entered the room. Not a word was spoken. My father, the wizard, went behind the desk and sat down. He then took a few books at a time and stacked them into piles, just giving him enough space so that he could write if need be. He folded his hands on the desk and looked right at me.

"I must tell you something, Cecil, before we begin."

He pointed to all of the piles of books on the desk. "See all of these books?"

I nodded.

"I have been working every evening this week, and haven't rested till the sun came up. I am a very tired wizard. I told you, Son, because I wanted you to know that I am working hard because of what your mother informed me of. I am talking about your dream. But I must tell you, I have an immediate situation."

My father had never told me about his business. He really must be exhausted.

"I sit before you, Son, to tell you about our latest problem. This one is separate from your dream. It has to do with our community. There is to be a meeting between the south side and the north side. Their mayor, chief of police and a lawyer will represent their side. And, your mother and I and our lawyer will represent our side. As far as your studies go, we will finish up Book One right now and get you going on Book Two. I didn't want to rush Book One, but I have no choice. I made up a chart that will track your success as you travel up the ladder to becoming a witch. I will show you that chart the next time we meet. Let's get started, because I have a lot to do."

This is a very good example of why I don't see my father that often. At least Billy, even though his life style is different than mine, still spends a lot of time with both of his parents. If he only knew, there are times that I envy him.

I answered all of the questions that my father asked me. Again, they were very easy to answer. I was told that Book Two would be a little bit harder, and Book Three would be even harder than Book Two, and so on and so on.

When I left my father's study, I turned around to see that he was going through the books as I walked out. With all that my father had told me about our neighbors, I still don't know why a meeting was called.

The last time a meeting was called, it had to do with a boundary dispute. The south claimed that, as a whole, both sides of the lake represented a town called Stoneway. At the time, they claimed that all of the property, even over the lake, belonged to them as well as the north. In other words, the town as a whole belonged to everyone. They, the south claimed that this separation was illegal. If I am not mistaken, this kind of meeting took place a very long time ago. I wouldn't be surprised if that is the reason why my parents have to go over to the south side. This meeting must be very important, for my parents have never been south of the lake. Well, as far as I know.

CHAPTER 8

In a few minutes, a meeting would begin on the south side of town. The mayor and the chief of police were sitting at a desk in a room at City Hall. Sitting in the audience was a group known as GOLB (Get Our Land Back). Their mission was to retrieve land back for the south side. I guess my suspicions were right about why this meeting had to be held.

Mr. Williams is the town mayor, and he was about to start the meeting.

"This meeting will come to order."

Mr. Williams looked the papers over. The audience was quiet. Not a word was being spoken.

"Will the representative from GOLB please stand up and state your case."

The representative from GOLB stood up. His name is Mr. Hyde.

"The people from GOLB have a problem with the fact that our town is divided by a lake, and that the north feels that they are entitled to more land over the lake."

"Mr. Hyde, as you and everyone else in this room knows, I am not a judge. I am the mayor of this town. We are here to discuss this problem, so don't expect some kind of a verdict out of this meeting. Is that understood, Mr. Hyde? And besides, we couldn't come to a conclusion if the other side isn't present to represent itself. Everyone has to be heard."

"Yes, Mr. Mayor."

"All right, then let's begin this meeting. Mr. Hyde, you may begin. Please step up to the microphone and tell us what you want."

"Mr. Mayor, we want our land back. It is as simple as that."

"No, it's not as simple as that, Mr. Hyde. How do you propose to get the land back?"

"We will take it if need be."

"Mr. Hyde, may I remind you that you are not dealing with ordinary people. You will not be able to just take the land that you feel you fully deserve. Rest assured, the Wizard of Stoneway will not allow this to happen."

"Mr. Mayor, the wizard is not the law in this town. We have rules and regulations."

"The problem is, they don't have the same rules and regulations, Mr. Hyde. May I refresh you memory? First of all, if you haven't noticed, on a nice sunny day, if you look up into the sky, you will find people flying around on their broomsticks. Mr. Hyde, I'm curious. Do you know what you're dealing with?"

"Mr. Mayor, the answer to your question is, yes. Our group has reviewed our stand on this situation and, might I say, our team of lawyers all concur. This land is not exclusively theirs. We are all entitled to live where we choose to live."

"Let me ask you a question, Mr. Hyde. How do you expect us to, as you say, take our so-called land back?"

"The law says that it is nobody's land exclusively."

"Mr. Hyde, have you tried crossing the bridge and talking to the wizard?"

"No."

"Don't you think that that would be the next step?"

"He doesn't particularly like our kind. We hung his people over 300 years ago and he blames everyone on the south side."

"I must tell you this, because I want you to know that I am going to have a meeting with the wizard tomorrow. That is why I wanted to know your situation, before I sit down with the wizard, his wife and a lawyer. The meeting will take place right in this room."

"You mean he is actually coming over here?"

"Yes, the first wizard in 300 years to do so. Am I actually going to let him come over here? Of course, I am going to let him come over here. Are you going to stop him?"

"Can my group be present during the meeting?"

"No, Mr. Hyde, the meeting will be private. I will have the chief of police, a lawyer and myself. This wizard can't be that unreasonable. He is coming over here. He could have said no to this meeting. Let's wait and see what the wizard has to say. I have a feeling that this meeting is going to be very interesting. I also believe that this meeting is now over."

Everyone was told to clear the room except for the chief of police and the mayor.

"Mr. Mayor, who asked for this meeting, tomorrow?" asked the chief of police.

"I did."

"How did you reach the wizard? I mean, how did you get the wizard to come here, on the south side?"

"After contacting him, I explained what the problem is over here, and what the people want. Let's just say, that I know the wizard."

"How do you know him?"

"I really don't want to discuss that just now. We must concentrate on tomorrow. It is indeed an historical day. The Wizard of Stoneway is coming to the south side. Not only is he the wizard, he is also the uncle of the Witch of London. He is a very powerful man. If Mr. Hyde were to confront the wizard, and he steps out of line, who knows? The wizard might turn him into whatever he wants to. So for the health and welfare of Mr. Hyde, I suspect that I did him a favor by not inviting him to this all important meeting."

"Mr. Mayor, how will we deal with the wizard? I mean, if he says no to this whole thing, it's pretty much over. I don't know about you, but I'm not one to argue with the most powerful man, the Wizard of Stoneway. I've personally seen what he can do. My parents have told me stories about how he helps his people. Mr. Mayor, do you know that they actually give money away to those who need it? Poverty doesn't exist in that part of town.

"Another story my parents told me was that about thirty years ago, the lake was just about dried up. The wizard went down to the lake, and stood on the edge of the tall grass that lines the lake's edge. There is where he cast a spell. The wizard raised both arms. He pointed his wand towards the sky. The next thing you knew, the lake was filled to the brim. Not only was it filled, the water was as clear and as smooth as glass. My parents also told me that fish could be seen jumping out of it. Thousands of fish were dancing on top of the water. The fish were so happy that they got their home back. The sun came out from behind a cloud, as if to smile to thank the wizard for what he had done. Is the meeting that will take place tomorrow going to accomplish anything, Mr. Mayor?"

"I believe that there's a 50/50 chance. It will all depend on the wizard. The question is, will he cooperate with us, or are we going to get a lecture on how things will be…and 'don't try and change them?'"

"Mr. Mayor, I keep asking myself the same questions. Why should the wizard cooperate? He knows that a lot of our people are afraid and probably, to some extent, jealous of the people from the north. I believe that there are few people who would move over to the north side of town. But, why would our people want to make that move?"

"Well, I believe it's just a matter of not wanting the north to occupy all of that land. You know, as well as I do, that we cannot live in total harmony with the north. The north side people really don't need us. What could we possible contribute to them? And besides, most of them don't care for us. So why move to a place where you are not welcome? Our people do not believe in their magic, or their way of life. I still don't see how anyone could question their magic. If you look up and see people flying around on their broomsticks, wouldn't you think that that would be enough proof that their magic works? Flying around on their broomsticks is their way of transportation. We see them every day. Yet, there are people who question their magical ways. It's beyond me."

"Well, I can hardly wait for this meeting to begin, tomorrow," said the chief of police.

"Neither can I. Neither can I."

CHAPTER 9

So the next day, my father, my mother and their lawyer took off into the skies over the north side of Stoneway. As they crossed over the lake, they slowly descended, as they got closer to the City Hall on the south side. From the air, they could see the mayor and his team walking up a road and into an open field where the south side team would greet them. My father and everyone else landed in the field and patiently waited for the mayor to approach them. As the mayor got close enough to the wizard, the mayor extended his hand. The wizard accepted the mayor's hand and they shook hands. History had just been made. No other wizard in history had even shaken hands with the Mayor of Stoneway. A matter of fact, no wizard had ever shaken hands with anyone from the south side.

"As the Mayor of Stoneway, I want to welcome all of you to the south side of Stoneway."

"Thank you Mr. Mayor, and I hope all is well."

The mayor nodded his head to assure the wizard that all was well with him and his immediate family.

"Can we get this started? I have a very important problem to take care of. It's my toughest problem to date."

"Sure, please follow me. I do hope that this problem can be solved," said the mayor.

"It has to be solved," answered the wizard.

Everyone else shook hands, and the proper introductions were finished. The mayor and the wizard walked side by side, while everyone else followed from behind.

From a distance, you could see the flash bulbs going off. Needless to say, the local newspapers now had their front-page pictures, to go along with their front-page stories. The people of the south side were kept at a distance during this whole trip. The people made comments about the way the royal couple dressed. Those people were too far away for my father to hear them…lucky for those people. You could tell that the wizard had a lot on his mind. His much larger problem was always on his mind. He thought about it every day from morning until he went to sleep. The wizard wanted more than anything to get this meeting over with and then head home to his study as quickly as possible.

While my parents were in the south, the south treated them like royalty. With my father and mother in the south side, there was no one here to run our community. I knew that I was too young for the job. I found out later that my cousin Stephen was on alert at a moment's notice. The one thing that my father wanted done before he left was to put some of his trusted witches up into the air, a handful of witches that would stay up for a few hours and then come down to rest. When they would get tired of flying, then a new group of witches would go up to replace those who were resting. They flew over the lake and into the south side territory, turning around just before City Hall and then returning over the lake. This pattern of flying was repeated until they got tired. The City Hall building is the closest building to the lake. No one lives near the lake…on either side. Between the lake and City Hall is a large open field. The field is about 400 yards long and about three miles wide.

The doors of City Hall opened and my parents were escorted into the building. The security in and around the building was very heavy. Once inside the building, they were led into a large room. The public was kept away from the building and no one entered City Hall that didn't belong there.

In the middle of the room was a rectangular table. It was perfect for this meeting, the three representatives from the south on one side, and the representatives from the north on the other side. The people from the south remained standing until everyone from the north was seated. The mayor then instructed his team to sit down. The mayor, after sitting down with his team, immediately stood up and spoke directly to the wizard, who was sitting across from him.

"Thank you so much for coming to this meeting."

The wizard just nodded his head. The wizard was also thinking about how many times this mayor had to thank him for showing up.

"Without wasting your time, I believe that I don't have to remind you why you are here," said the mayor.

The wizard pushed his chair back and then stood up. The mayor immediately sat down. Now the wizard was looking directly into the mayor's eyes.

"This meeting is a total waste of everyone's time. Let me explain. The only reason I am here is because I want this settled once and for all. First of all, my people were here over 300 hundred years ago when your people were just arriving. And no sooner had they arrived than they were hanging our people. How is it that your people live on the south side of the lake? I'll tell you why. Winston Longstreet, a relative of mine, founded this territory, better known as Stoneway. He was the first wizard in this area as well. What he had in mind was a vision. This vision gave his people a place to live. As time went on, your people showed up and my grandfather, who had a heart of gold, allowed your people to live on the property south of the lake. He told them that they could stay as long as they had to. To show Winston their gratitude, they started to hang our people. Winston took care of the problem. He did allow the innocent to continue to live in the south. He did not give this land to those people. Let me repeat that. He did not give them the land. In order to give them responsibilities and a sense of pride, he charged them rent. They were to work the land and grow crops of all sorts. The rent he charged was so little, he made sure that it wasn't a burden for anyone. After his untimely death, his will was read. The will mentioned that these people could still live on the land. It specifically said that they didn't own the land. They were to continue to rent. The land always belonged to my people, and it will always belong to my people. Mr. Mayor, your people are visitors who were allowed to live on the land because Winston Longstreet felt sorry for them. Somewhere along the line, your people stopped paying rent. Ever since they stopped paying rent they have felt that they own the property. We don't collect the rent, and we haven't collected it for a few centuries. Your people for some reason started paying into your banks. Phony papers were also made up along the way, giving your people false hope for owning property. The problem with that was that they were fooled. The other problem was, that no one ever told them that that piece of paper, know as a deed, is worthless. They really thought they were paying the banks monthly so that after a while they would own the house they live in outright. It's all a very big scam. And your people don't know it."

The mayor looked at his lawyer and then back to the wizard. Everyone at the table from the south had a look of puzzlement. The mayor didn't know what to say. Silence fell upon the room, a silence that seemed to go on for a very long time.

"I really don't know what to say, at least not now. But I do have a question for you," said the mayor.

The wizard sat down and the mayor stood up.

"How did your people wind up north of the lake? Why not the south side?"

"A good question, but yet a very simple question. Winston Longstreet wanted his people closer to Stonehenge. Without going into details, Stonehenge is very dear to us. It means a lot to us. Let me ask you a question, Mr. Mayor."

Now the mayor sat down and the wizard remained seated.

"Why, all of a sudden, are your people interested in land on the north side?"

"Before I continue, I want to make a point. I want you to know that it isn't all of us that want to expand. You do realize that a percentage of our people are extremely afraid of anyone who is living in the north. They're not into all of the magic. Besides, looking skyward and seeing people flying around on their broomsticks sends them running for their homes. The people who want to expand to the north are not afraid of your people. It's not as if they want to become friends, but they would like more acreage around their houses. And let's face it, you do have miles and miles of open fields."

This time, the wizard's lawyer got up from his seat. "Excuse me, Mr. Mayor. The wizard has to get back to his study. Are there any more questions for the wizard? If not, we must be leaving."

Now the chief of police got up from his chair and looked right at the lawyer.

"Don't you think that the wizard will leave when the time is right? Who are you to interfere?"

The wizard put his right hand up toward his lawyer's face, to stop him from answering.

"Gentlemen, it is almost time for me to get back. I must get back, but there are a few things that have to be discussed before I leave. You can go back and tell your people that they will not be coming over to the north side of the lake. That's the first thing. The second thing that you can tell your people is not to try and accumulate land over the lake. It will never happen as long as I am alive. And the third thing you can tell them is that they should feel very lucky that they were given the privilege of living in the south, dirt cheap, by a warm-hearted wizard. It was a wizard who felt sorry for them and opened his land to them. Tell them that and see what they have to say to you. I see that you also brought your lawyer. What kinds of papers did you bring? I would like to see them."

The lawyer opened his brief case and a bunch of papers flew into the hands of the queen.

"Husband, I believe that you should look at these papers." The queen handed the papers to her husband. The wizard took them, but hardly glanced at them. After a few seconds, he turned to the mayor.

"Mr. Mayor, where did you get these papers?"

"From the records department in the basement of this building. Why, what's wrong?"

"These papers are copies of a proposal from the late 1800s. It's not even an agreement! I hope that you were not expecting me to just say, sure, take all the land you want. You know that both the north and the south can live in peace. I hope you didn't think that that is what I was going to say. Before I forget, that proposal was just another attempt to obtain land. Trying to take land from us has been going on for a very long time. So, as you can see, you are not the first generation to try."

"We were hoping that you would be in a generous mood. The people would pay you for the land."

"Mr. Mayor, money is one thing that we don't need any more of. We have other ways to make money."

"What if I told you that if you would let go of some acreage, my people would agree to a peace treaty?"

"Mr. Mayor, I cannot consider that, even for a second. I know how your people feel about us. It would never work. Too much bad blood throughout the centuries."

"But all of those people are not around. Wouldn't you consider our offer just on that fact? At least think it over. Many generations have come and gone, but this generation favors a treaty. Please, think about it, for me."

"For you, I will consider it. You have never lied to me. But, don't get your hopes up."

"Okay," agreed the mayor.

"I must leave now. I have pressing matters awaiting me in my study."

The mayor extended his hand, as did everyone else. The wizard's party was escorted out. Away they flew, once they were off the front steps of City Hall. Everyone was back in the north in a few minutes.

As the wizard's party headed back to the house, the witches who were flying around waved to them as they flew by.

Once the wizard returned home safely, the flying witches left the sky. The wizard went straight back to his study. The queen went into the kitchen to throw a meal together... literally. The lawyer, well, he just went back to his house. He is the official royal lawyer. He is always on call. The lawyer doesn't receive a large salary, but he does get a lot of privileges. One of them is that he gets his house for free. Lawyers and other professionals always got their houses for free, with a low salary. It's been that way for centuries. The wizard wanted to keep that tradition going.

Now the wizard had other things on his mind besides traditions. He went as far as to lock the doors that led into his study. The almighty powerful wizard, the most powerful man in this territory, wanted to be alone. For the first time in his life, he was very unsure of himself.

I must focus. Too many people depend on me.

CHAPTER 10

While my father was busy in his study, I was in the kitchen with my mother.

"Cecil, did you forget what holiday is coming up, and you never said a thing about it to me?"

I thought for a second. "You know, you're right, mother. The one holiday that pertains to us and it slipped my mind."

"That's right. It's called the Festival of the Royals. Don't you remember, that's when the people in our community dress up like us and celebrate the founding of Stoneway," said the queen.

"But Mother, will Father appear as he always has, knowing how busy he is?"

"I have spoken to your father, and he has assured me that he will not disappoint his people. He will be there, if only for a short while, but he will be there."

"This festival will be starting in two days. So that's why I am seeing booths being set up and signs hanging from trees."

"Right. In two days, all of the stores will be closed and everyone in the community will participate either by marching in the parade or manning a booth of some kind. I remember the booth from last year that you enjoyed so much. Don't you remember that booth, Cecil?"

"I remember that booth. I finally managed to bite into an apple and drag it out of the barrel. By the time I did, I was soaked. Everyone was cheering me on. It was a great time for all. Not too sure if I will try that again."

"By the way, Cecil, your father wants you and your book in his study before lunch."

"Thanks, I know."

I looked at the clock on the wall and I figured out that I had just enough time to get my book and be at my father's study on time.

I arrived on time. I knocked on the door, no answer. I tried the doorknob. It was locked. This time I knocked harder.

"Yes."

Finally, my father answered. I could hear my father walking towards the door. The door opened. I looked up at this enormous figure of a man looking down at me.

"Come in, Son. I must have dozed off."

He looked at my book, then, and remembered why I was there.

"I can see that you are ready for Book Two. Well, come in and sit down."

My father went behind his desk so that he could sit down. I probably woke him up, but how was I to know he was sleeping?

We went through Book Two much faster than Book One. I passed my test with flying colors. My father told me that we would start Book Three after the Festival of the Royals.

My father took my book and threw it back into its original slot on the bookshelf. Book Three moved itself out of the shelf and dropped off and flew towards me. Then I caught it. It still amazes me. I can hardly wait to be able to do that magic myself.

My father reached around to the side of his desk and pulled a large piece of cardboard out. All I saw from where I was standing were a lot of boxes. It was my progress report. I was right. When I saw it close up, there were a lot of boxes, so many boxes, I couldn't count them. Looking at the progress chart reminded me of all the work that was ahead of me. I really didn't know how, once I got back to school, I would be able to handle my schoolwork and my witch-in-training work. I would just have to put my mind into it and do it, that's all.

After leaving my father's study, I headed to my library. Once there, I put my book on my desk, and I faced my bookshelf. I only have hundreds of books; my father has thousands. I eyed a book on the top shelf and, in my mind, asked for that book to pull itself from the shelf and come to me. I kept looking at the book. It didn't budge. I just thought that I would give it a try.

I have no idea what my father says to himself to make those books fly off the shelf. Waiting has never been one of my strengths. I know that I will have to wait years before I will have that kind of power.

Turning around, I sat down at my desk. Glancing through Book Three, I realized that this book would be much harder to go through. It would all be well worth it…I kept telling myself that.

I looked through a few more pages and then put the book down. My full concentration was now on the up and coming festival. I couldn't understand how this important holiday had completely slipped my mind.

Tomorrow would be a good day to read a few chapters, not taking too much time for studying, and then to see who needed my help in the community.

I left my library and went downstairs. When I got to the bottom of the stairs, I could hear my mother calling for me.

"Cecil!"

"Mother, I am right here."

"I thought you were still upstairs."

"What do you want, Mother?"

"I want to tell you that Henry and Charles have just arrived. I had them sit and wait for you in the music room."

Anyone in the community is allowed to come to our house. Some people call this house a mansion. "House" is so much cozier.

The music room is a room that is near the front door, but off to the left, if you're facing the house. My mother and I play the piano when we have time. Our queen also gives music lessons to those who request them, free of charge, of course. We must have 10 different instruments. The violins outnumber all of the other instruments. On the other side of the piano, there is a drum set. When my parents leave the house, I get behind the drums and play my little heart out.

I went into the music room to greet my friends.

"Henry, Charles, nice to see the both of you."

"Cecil, Henry and I wanted to know if the future prince would come out and help us with our booth?"

"Well boys, I was going to study my book tomorrow and then go out and help anyone who needed help. I guess I could start today. Do you have all your tools that you will need? What kind of a game did you have in mind for your booth?"

"It was Charles's idea. We call it 'Hole In One.' We have to get burlap and sand. We are going to make small sand bags. We also have to get sewing needles and thread. The idea is to throw at least two out of three sand bags through a hole. If they can do that, we give them a small prize.

Of course, everything is free. By the way, there will be a drawing of our wizard on the board. We are going to cut out his mouth. The mouth will be the target. Pretty good, huh?"

"My father will find that funny."

"Well, that's good to hear," said Henry. "In the past, people have donated material to build the booths and have even given us toys to give out as prizes. Cecil, you know that a lot of the kids dress as you. This year, I am going to dress like you. How do you feel when you see someone dressed like you?"

"To tell you the truth, it's embarrassing. After I see this for a while, I start to laugh. All in good fun. I think we should start to gather everything that we need and head for the area where we will set up."

The area that I am talking about is down by the lake. There's a section there that has been used for the last 50 years. All booths are set up there. The parade will start by my house and end by the lake. Once there, everyone enters the area of the booths. There are also booths just for food. They can be found scattered about the grounds in no special order.

Every household in the community either cooks or bakes something. With all of the preparing that has to be done, not a penny is spent, and not a penny is earned. We pride ourselves on that. The horse farms donate the horses for the parade. The horses pull the floats made by the people in the community. I understand that my cousin, Stephen, the Wizard of London, will be leading the parade this year. He is such a fun guy. Someday, I would like to have his job.

When the festival starts, you can see the curious people from the south looking over towards us having a good time. I only hope that someday the South can join in and celebrate with us.

My friends and I accomplished a lot that day. Henry and Charles made sand bags and I drew a portrait of my father and cut a hole where the mouth would be. I must say, I did a fine job. After the booth was set up and the game was put into its place, Henry, Charles and myself, played for at least an hour. It was so much fun.

While we were putting our booth together, I looked around to see that everyone was working together, helping each other and, most important of all, having a wonderful time.

Meanwhile, a few miles north of the lake, floats were being put together at a farm owned by Mr. and Mrs. Williams. Once a float is completed, it is taken out of the barn and placed in the corral where the horses are kept during the day. The work then continues again, inside the barn, on the next float.

I was told that the committee had chosen a theme that is quite different from last year's theme. Last year's theme was based on the life of our founder, Winston Longstreet. Since this festival takes place because of Winston Longstreet, the committee felt that it was only fitting that floats should be built around his life. This year, the theme is based on my family's life. Some of the floats will show how we all help each other. It's about helping our neighbors and our own families.

The Williams family has been helping us for years, well, ever since I can remember. The family consists of six children, a mother and a father. Between them all, these floats are built at a rapid pace. The Williams family also donates the horses that pull these floats.

After Henry, Charles and I finished playing, we went over to the Williams farm to see if we could lend a hand.

I walked up to Mr. Williams. It's been a while since I'd spoken to him.

"Hello, Mr. Williams."

"Cecil, whom do I thank for this honor?"

"Oh, Mr. Williams. My friends and I are here to help you with the floats."

"Well, if you look around, you can see that I have more help than I can use. You're welcome to wait around until I need you, but really, maybe you would be more helpful at another workstation. Don't get me wrong, it was nice of you boys to ask, but I have more than enough help. Thanks, anyway."

"You're welcome. But who do you think could use us?" asked Henry.

Mr. Williams thought and thought.

"I have an idea, boys. Why don't you three work on your own float?"

The three of us just looked at each other and we all answered at once.

"Yes!" Brilliant, we all thought.

"You boys can use the far left corner of the barn to build your float. All the materials that you will need are against the wall. If you need my help, just call me over." One of the rules for building floats is to not use your magical powers. If magic could be used, these floats would all be built in no time. By the way, that rule also goes for building booths.

"Thank you so much, Mr. Williams," said Charles.

Mr. Williams walked over to the corner where the boys would be working. He pointed to an already made frame with the four wheels already attached.

"I was going to use what you are about to work on, but as you can see, I have already set the wheels in place and I have already built the floor of the float. All you boys have to do is set your exhibit up, and tie it to the floor, put sides on it, hitch the horse up and we will be ready for tomorrow's parade. As a matter of fact, if it's all right with your parents, Cecil, how would you like to ride the horse that will pull your float in the parade?"

"I will check with my parents, but I see no reason why I can't ride the horse in the parade. Thank you for allowing me this opportunity."

"Just let me know. This way, we can give the honors to Henry or Charles."

"Okay, I'll let you know."

Henry, Charles and I had to think about what kind of float we would build. They came up with several ideas, but which one should we choose?

"I like your idea, Charles," I said.

"Thanks, but I really like Henry's idea," said Charles.

"And we also like your idea, Cecil," said Henry.

"I got it, why don't we combine all three ideas on one float?" I said.

"Brilliant, Cecil," Charles chimed in.

Henry nodded slowly. "Absolutely brilliant," he said.

So all of us gathered up all of the materials that we needed. Then we all started to work on our separate ideas. Because it was early in the morning, there was still plenty of time left in the day to finish the float.

About midway through the work, Mr. Williams called from across the room, "Are you boys doing okay? Need anything?"

"No, thanks," I called back. We're fine. Thanks for all the materials."

Even though the festival was the next day, a lot had already been accomplished by most of the community. After three hours, we were ready to nail our projects to the floor of our float.

We stood back and admired our handiwork. It was beautiful, and it would be different from any other float.

"Nice job, guys," I said.

"Thanks," said Henry.

"Thanks," said Charles.

CHAPTER 11

There are people who have worked through the night. There was a full moon last night, so a lot of light shown down on Stoneway. This community is like a chain. All of the links are very strong. No matter how much you pull on it, they will all hold, and never break apart. You might be thinking, how can so many people trust each other and help each other? The answer is very simple…we do it to survive. If we don't help each other, who will?

I jumped out of bed and ran down the stairs in my pajamas. My mother and father met me in the kitchen.

"Cecil, why did you come downstairs in your pajamas?" asked his mother.

"Mother, I guess that I am so excited about today, I just ran down the stairs to get breakfast, and didn't waste time dressing."

"You might as well have breakfast. You are already here," my father said.

A bowl appeared before him with cereal and milk already in it. A spoon came out of the drawer and flew into the bowl. Oh, how I wish I could do that.

"Mother, Father. Henry, Charles and I built our own float yesterday over at the Williams farm. Mr. Williams wants to know, with your permission, if I can ride the horse that pulls our float?"

"What is the theme of your float?" asked my father.

"It's a surprise, Father."

"Okay, I guess we'll have to wait," said my mother.

"You'll see. I believe that you will really like it. So, can I ride the horse?"

"Yes, you may ride the horse. But not until after the opening ceremonies," my father replied.

After finishing breakfast, I ran back up the stairs to get myself ready. I opened my enormous closet, which is full of colorful clothes. All of the people in the community wear colorful clothes as well. They only do this to show respect to their leaders.

I took out the outfit that I was going to wear and spread it out on the bed. It consisted of my pants, jacket and a shirt. Walking over to my dresser, I took out a pair of bright purple socks and put these socks into my yellow shoes. Next, I took out my yellow underwear and my purple undershirt. Now that I had collected everything that I needed to dress, I realized that I was missing one item, the hat. When I become a witch, I will earn the right to wear it. Right now, my hair is not that long, but someday, I hope to have hair as long as my father's.

Once dressed, I met my parents at the front door. The royal family was now dressed and ready for the ceremonies to begin. Someone will come to the front door and open it from the outside, where the crowds have been gathering all morning. Once the door is opened, we will begin our walk, and the festival will be considered officially started. This festival only lasts one day. There used to be a time when this festival lasted for three days. Three days of drinking, dancing, and mischief. One of the wizards put a stop to all of that many years ago.

"Remember, Husband...smile, no matter how heavy your load. Our people want to see you and meet you. Please, don't let on that something is wrong. Why spoil their day? You know that they adore you. Don't let them down."

"I will smile, and I will greet the people of our community."

I jumped in and said, "And I'll be right behind you."

I had a lot on my mind as well. I was very anxious to get to my horse and at the same time, I had not forgotten about my dream. It didn't bother me as much as before, only because I had faith in my father, who told me that he would take care of the problem. Knowing that lightened my load.

Time grew near, and the front door began to open, ever so slowly. At the first sign of daylight through the small crack of the opening door, the sound of trumpets could be heard. It was a sound suitable only for royalty. It was the sound that introduced the royal family of Stoneway to the community.

As my family walked down to the crowds, trumpeters were lined up on both sides of the walk. My father the wizard, my mother the queen and I, a future witch, walked slowly down the many steps. The people came to see their leaders, clapping and yelling out to us.

"We love you! We love you!"

My parents walked over to the orderly crowds with their heads held high, shook their hands and talked to the ones that asked them questions, or told them how great they were. The majority of them thanked my parents for all they had done. Even though my father has a real stubborn streak in him, he has, deep down inside of him, a heart of gold. It's the stubborn part of him that bothers me.

Looking out into the crowd, you couldn't help but notice all of the costumes, so many people looking like me and like the members of my family. As we continued to walk along the path lined with people, I was wondering how long it would be till I could ride that horse.

"Cecil."

"Yes, Mother."

"Continue to wave at the people and stop thinking about anything else."

"Was it that obvious?"

"Yes, yes it was," said the Queen.

I noticed that once my father got to the end of the long walk, he turned around and walked back to the house.

He looked back at my mother and me.

"Continue on. I must get back. Have a great time!"

And so we did.

"Mother, I must get to the floats before the parade starts up."

"All right, be careful. Enjoy yourself."

I ran as fast as my little legs would carry me. If only I could have flown.

Henry and Charles met me at the Williams farm.

"Cecil, nice to see you. We have a couple of minutes to go before we line up all the floats. Aren't you excited?" asked Henry.

"Yes, sure, Henry, I am very excited. Can hardly wait."

"I sure hope that everyone likes our float. It is different, you know," said Charles.

"Charles, slow down, you're going to hurt yourself," I said.

I hitched up the horse to the float and hopped on the horse's back. I turned around and gave my mates instructions.

"Okay, get on the float and hold on. Don't need anyone falling off."

The boys listened to me and then hopped on, each taking his position. We then rode off toward the far end of the property where Mr. Williams was lining up all of the floats.

As we approached the area, we finally noticed Mr. Williams.

"Cecil, will you please pull behind Ms. Sherman's float. You are number eight in line."

I thought about our position in line: number eight. Why? I suppose that it has to do with the fact that I am not yet royalty. I waved to Mr. Williams, giving him the sign that I understood.

"Cecil," called Henry, "you know Ms. Sherman has a nice daughter, don't you?"

"Do you mean to tell me that that's Becky's mother?"

"Yes, yes it is."

"She looks nothing like her mother," I answered.

"Thank goodness," said Charles. We had a good laugh over that.

After waiting about half an hour, the floats actually started to move. The main street was full of the population of Stoneway…from the north side. People were waving and shouting. Some even shouted out "Happy Birthday" to us.

By the time the eighth float showed up, the crowd was out of control. They were so excited to see a member of the royal family. The clapping and shouting got louder and they began chanting, "Cecil, Cecil, Cecil."

This, of course, embarrassed me very much. I thought that I could handle this, but I was indeed uncomfortable. I waved to the crowd, as did Charles and Henry. As they got closer, the crowd noticed, now in full view, the float in all its grandeur. Now, the shouting suddenly subsided down to a low roar and the clapping practically stopped. It was as if someone had taken the air out of a balloon. The crowd was studying the float, examining the objects on it. Some didn't quite know what to make of it.

"Henry, can you see the looks on the faces of these people? Very few are even waving at us. What did we do wrong?"

"Charles, think about it. The float tells of a future where man has no enemies. It tells of a future when everyone can live together in peace. Don't you get it?"

"You mean, the people of the south?"

"Yes, most of our people don't want that peace. Whatever happened over 300 years ago has not yet been forgotten."

"Henry, people don't forget, and today is no exception. Just look straight ahead, and pray that nothing is thrown at us."

As the parade advanced towards the lake area, the cheering and shouting and waving got less and less. The noise level got so low, you would have thought that it was a funeral. The boys and I just followed Ms. Sherman's float and all we wanted was for this to end now. This was turning out to be, and will probably go down in history, as the worst parade ever in the town of Stoneway.

As if that wasn't bothering me enough, how about the thought of facing my parents! How was I supposed to walk around town? Every time I am seen in public, someone will say, "There goes the boy who ruined our holiday parade."

My mates and I have managed to upset a great percentage of the population. Trying to make a statement is very risky, especially when the majority of the town does not agree with you.

We finally made it to the holding area where all of the floats were parked.

I remembered last year's parade when people were gathered around our float and they continued to wave and cheer. This year, two people showed up, two young lads. They stood facing the float and clapped till their hands hurt. The two small boys had no idea what they were looking at.

"Boys, thank you so much. Now, please join your friends at the booth area," I said.

The boys ran off, which left the area around the float deserted. We could see Mr. Williams approaching our float, and he didn't look happy. Henry and Charles jumped off the back of the float and walked to the front, where they joined me. Now we were standing, waiting for Mr. Williams to give us some kind of lecture. It was difficult to read Mr. Williams face, so we all waited patiently for him.

"Good morning, boys, and congratulations."

"Congratulating us, are you?" said Henry.

"No, you twit!" Then he turned to me. "Pardon, Cecil."

"Oh, no, that's okay. It is going to be much more severe for me when I get back to my house, or as soon as the news reaches my parents. Whichever comes first."

"I will be as calm as I can be. You boys are lucky that Cecil is with you, or I might lose it," said Mr. Williams.

"We were just stating a fact and a hope for the future, that's all, Mr. Williams," said Henry.

"You know, I didn't check your float. I trusted all of you to use good sense on this. You had to use this parade for your stage. This is a celebration. We are celebrating our town and its founder. If you haven't realized it yet, Henry and Charles, hundreds of people are dressed up in yellow pants and such. What did you think this parade was about?"

"Mr. Williams, I have to take the responsibility as well."

"No, Cecil, I do not blame you."

"Mr. Williams, I appreciate your loyalty towards my family, but I was also involved in this plan, and I should not be left out of the blame. I am just as guilty. The theme included ideas from all three of us."

"Well, it was the wrong thing to do." Mr. Williams waved to me and just looked at Henry and Charles as he turned and walked away. It's anyone's guess what he would have done if I hadn't been here. Henry and Charles thanked me for standing by them.

"To the booths, gentlemen," I said. I pointed toward the booth area and the boys left, heading that way.

I had changed my mind about joining my mates. Henry and Charles looked to their sides and realized that I wasn't with them.

"Cecil, aren't you going to join us?"

"No, you two enjoy yourselves. I have something to take care of. Go ahead, play."

CHAPTER 12

"What were you bloody thinking?" yelled the wizard. The wizard was circling the chair that I was sitting in, never taking his eyes off me.

"Sir, I came to you to tell you the truth."

"That was very honorable of you. Of course you know that that doesn't change anything. The damage is already done. You and your friends ruined the parade."

"Damage?"

"Yes, damage," said the wizard.

"My mates and I had no idea that this would happen. We were stating a theme...."

"It certainly wasn't in keeping with the theme of the parade!"

"We had no idea that this would cause such controversy. We only wanted to get a message out to the people, maybe put hope into them about the future where everyone can live together."

"Live together! You mean live together with those people across the lake? What has gotten into you and your friends? Do you honestly believe that everyone can live in harmony? Name a country that has complete harmony!"

"We're not talking about harmony amongst a country, we're talking about living amongst our neighbors."

"There is not a town in this country where everyone gets along. You are so young in your ways, my son. Not everybody gets along with their neighbors...complete harmony...never."

"So you believe that we will never live in harmony with our neighbors across the lake?"

"Never."

"You know what they say, Father. Never say never."

The wizard stopped circling the chair that I was sitting in. He looked me straight in the eyes and continued to lecture.

"In my lifetime, the people on the other side of the lake will...never live amongst us. Is that understood?"

"I have never disrespected you, have I, Father?"

"Are you counting today?"

"In the past. Although, this was not done to intentionally show you disrespect."

"No, no you haven't."

"I will always think of ways to join the North with the South. Someday, and this is a vision and dream of mine, someday people will be walking back and forth over that bridge. I will rename that bridge The Bridge of Freedom."

"And when do you expect to do all of this?

"Someday, Father, someday."

"Well, that's all well and good, and you keep having those dreams...but not in my lifetime."

"Who knows, Father, who knows?"

The wizard walked to his desk and sat down. He pointed to me and demanded my attention. The tone of the wizard's voice had changed.

"Listen to me! Look directly into my eyes!" The wizard pointed to his own eyes. "You and your friends have done something today that, as far as I am concerned, ruined a very happy occasion. You must be punished, and I believe I have the perfect punishment for you."

"Being punished for what I believe?"

"Believe what you want. You had my people scattering from the parade grounds, and running back to their houses to hide. Wouldn't you say that you did something to scare them?"

"They are actually scared of peace. Don't you find that to be silly, Father?"

"What I find silly is that fact that three young boys thought they were going to change a history of over 300 years with a parade!"

"We saw no harm, we meant no harm."

"You will immediately start your punishment. You will also delay your studies toward being a witch."

"What do you want me to do?"

"First off, your friends' parents will be visited and brought over to me. While that is going on, you will be staying with your cousin, the Witch of London."

"That's my punishment?"

"Your cousin has been informed of your duties and you will obey him. It might even help you on your road to becoming a witch."

"You said that my punishment starts immediately."

The doorbell rang, its beautiful chimes a melody suited to a king.

"Answer the door, Cecil."

I got out of my chair and walked to the front door. Once there, I slowly opened it. Being that the wizard has an open door policy, it could be anyone ringing the doorbell. The wizard knew who it was.

Once the door was opened wide, it was obvious who it was. "Hello, Cecil. Coming to live with me?"

"Hello, Cousin Stephen. Won't you come in? Don't tell me. My father is expecting you?"

"A mind reader as well. Powerful stuff. Where is your father?"

"He's in his study. I'll walk you there."

I led the way, even though I knew that my cousin knew the way to my father's study. Once at the door, I knocked and waited for my father to reply.

"Come in."

I led the way and introduced my cousin to my father.

"Cousin Stephen, meet my father, the wizard."

"Cecil, have you lost it? Of course I know Stephen. Have known him since he was born. Cecil, you may leave. I will call for you right after this meeting."

I left the room and headed for my study. I could still hear them talking as I continued my walk through the hallway.

"Why did he introduce me to you? Strange, that one," commented Stephen.

"Listen, Stephen, I want to discuss some last minute concerns with you, and…."

Their voices faded as I walked farther along the hallway. As I turned the corner at the end of the hallway, there was nothing but silence from the direction of my father's study.

Someone was knocking on my door. The door started to open.

"Hello, may I come in?"

"Sure, Mum, come in."

"I understand that you will be staying with your cousin for a while."

"Yes, I am being punished."

"Well, you did upset a lot of people. People who are not ready for that kind of a drastic change."

"What my friends and I did was an idea. It was a dream for a brighter future. A future that lets everyone live together in peace."

"Those people don't want that change. We don't want that change. The people from the south side have nothing to contribute to our society."

"You and my father are missing the point."

"And what point is that?"

"It's not what those people can contribute, it's about everyone living together in peace. Did you know that recently my father has ordered that anyone who tries to cross the bridge into the south is to be immediately locked up and the key thrown away?"

"Dear, your father is protecting our land."

"From whom? Those people can't fly. They don't and can't perform an ounce of magic. They don't even believe in our magic. What could they possibly do to us?"

"I will not continue with this conversation. If your father knew we were talking about this subject, he wouldn't like it."

"What would he do to you? Aren't you allowed to express your opinion? Now you see what treatment you get from a man who is close-minded and who can't even put aside the fact that something happened over 300 years ago. And those people living on the south side today had nothing to do with it!"

My mother turned around and hurried out of my room. I don't know what got into me, but all I know is, I have a birthday coming up next week, and I hope I make it to the age of 11.

Another knock on my door.

"Come in."

"Hello, Cecil."

"Oh, hi. Come in, Cousin Stephen."

Stephen was all dressed up, wearing his yellow pants, red shirt and purple cape. He had removed his yellow pointed hat when he entered the house and had not as yet put it back on his head.

"Cecil, I was asked to come and bring you back to my place. Gather up a few articles and we'll be on our way."

"Give me a few minutes. You might as well take a seat."

"I have some people back at my place who want to meet you, so let's get a move on."

I grabbed a suitcase, threw a few things into it, and led Cousin Stephen to the front door. At the front door, I stopped and turned around to face my parents.

"I'm going now. I just wanted you to know that this punishment will in no way change my mind. You are both wasting your time."

No response from my parents.

So I walked alongside my cousin, who had decided not to take the vehicle. There is a road that goes from the front of my house and continues towards the back through the property and into the grounds of the largest house anyone has ever set their eyes on.

As we approached the Witch of London's property, we were greeted by two very small men. Stephen and I stopped walking and started talking.

"Cecil, these are just a few of the small people that are very anxious to meet you."

I looked down at the small person at my side.

"He doesn't look like he's happy to greet me. Cousin Stephen, these are gnomes. You have gnomes as helpers? Why haven't I ever seen them before?"

"They don't go over the line. They don't go off the property."

I looked down and finally I saw the line that my cousin was talking about. I pointed to the line.

"There. There's the line. An actual line in the grass."

Cousin Stephen pointed to one of the gnomes.

"Take his bag into the house. His room will be on the third floor, room 302. Where are my manners? Cecil, this gnome's name is Gotam. He will take your luggage to your room.

I got on one knee to shake his hand. Each gnome is approximately 18 inches high.

"Glad to make your acquaintance. I'm Cecil." The gnome just nodded his head.

"Not a friendly guy, is he?"

"He nodded his head. That means he's excited. And this gnome's name is Motam. He's one of my personal assistants. If I need a bodyguard, he's it."

I pointed to Motam. "He's a bodyguard? Have you gone daft?"

"Shake his hand, Cecil."

I walked up to Motam and knelt down on one knee and he extended his hand. Motam grabbed my hand, knocking me off balance, and I fell to the ground. As I did so, I began to laugh in surprise. Motam walked over to me and offered to pick me up.

"He wants to pick me up off of the ground. He can't do that, can he?"

"They're very strong, Cecil. They are 11 times stronger than we are. Don't ask me why or how that can happen, I don't know."

I thanked Motam, but picked myself up from the ground.

"Don't let their size fool you. Another thing, all of the gnomes are very dedicated to me. They will do whatever I want them to do. They are a very loyal bunch."

"How many gnomes do you have?"

"At last count, I had 125 gnomes, and they all have jobs to do at and around my house."

"How did they come to serve you?"

"Good question."

I studied Motam. I noticed that he was standing as straight as a soldier. Motam was standing just before the line in the grass. He was guarding the property. Cousin Stephen and I begin our walk to the main house.

"When I became the Witch of London, the gnomes came with the house. The story goes like this. Winston, while traveling around the world, brought back a total of

30 gnomes from various places like, Ireland, Romania and Spain. Now, some gnomes have as many as 15 children. They all work around here. See Motam over there? His wife works in the kitchen. His 10 children cut the lawn. Granted, it takes them two and a half days to cut the grass, but they are very loyal to me. They only want to make me happy. They will cut the grass till the job is finished. That means working by moonlight and into the next day if need be."

"So there are many generations working here?

"Yes, and they will continue to do so."

"Why don't they run away? Surely there has to be at least one or two that don't want to hang around."

"They couldn't if they tried."

"How is that possible?"

"Old Winston put a spell on the original gnomes, and that spell has spread to the future generations."

"Can't you undo the spell?"

"Since Winston is no longer around, nobody knows the exact spell that he used. Therefore, we don't know how to undo it. There are just too many combinations of spells to deal with. Anyway, this is the life that they are accustomed to. They are treated very well here. If I released them, if I was able to, where would they go? Now, releasing them would be the cruel thing to do. Anyway, I can't undo what Winston did, so they continue to work here. Here we are. We have arrived."

As we approached the huge front door, a gnome opened it. Stephen looked down.

"Thank you, Samar," said Stephen.

"You're very welcome, sir."

Once inside, Stephen told me that he wanted me to go to my room escorted by a gnome, so that I would not get lost.

"Fix up your room so that you are comfortable and then come downstairs and meet me in my office."

"How will I know where your office is?"

"As soon as you step into the hallway, a gnome will be there to escort you to my office. I told you, every gnome has a job. Some jobs are more important than others. One of the rules of this house, nobody walks around unescorted."

A gnome showed up to escort me to my room.

"Baten, please take our visitor to his room. Room 302."

So off we went, heading for somewhere on the third floor. I stopped and turned around.

"Stephen, do they all wear white beards and a pointed hat?"

"Only the men."

I turned around and continued the journey up to my room.

CHAPTER 13

"Come in."

As a gnome opened the huge door for me, I saw Stephen sitting at the largest desk you can ever imagine. As I walked towards the desk, I let Stephen know how I felt about this huge room.

"Cousin Stephen, I know that my house isn't considered to be a small house, but this room…." I touched the desk, running my fingers over the designs that had been carved directly into the top of the oak desk.

"Cecil, this room is one of the smaller rooms in the house."

"You're kidding."

"No, I'm not kidding."

Stephen pointed to the chair that he wanted me to sit in.

"Cecil, please take a seat. Sit down and relax. Now, please explain to me, in your own words, why you are here."

"You mean you don't know?"

"I talked to your father. Yes, I do know. I just want to hear it from you."

"I'm here because my two friends, Henry and Charles, and I, decided to make a point."

"And?"

"Our float was not well received by the community."

"What kind of float was it?"

"The float represented freedom and the hope that maybe someday, people would be able to live together in peace. I was thinking more on the lines of the people from the south living in peace with us. My father does not agree with that ever happening. Not in his lifetime."

"Is that what he said?"

"Yes."

"And that's why you got punished?"

"Yes."

"Well, I was going to discuss this with you tomorrow, but I have decided to tell you this now."

"Tell me what?"

"I have to tell you that you are not here because you are being punished. The truth is, you are not being punished."

"What! I don't understand. But my father said…."

"Listen to me carefully. I have no reason to lie to you. You are not being punished."

"My father said…."

Stephen got up from his huge chair. He put both of his hands on the desk and then leaned forward toward me.

"Cecil, bloody listen! You are not being punished."

"Then why am I here? And more important, why did my father lie to me?"

"It is true that you did scare a lot of people with your float. It is true that your father wasn't happy with what you and your mates did. But the truth is…even though your father isn't happy about the type of float that you made, he is very proud that you stood up for what you believe."

"Okay, this is getting confusing. He's mad at me, but he is proud of me?"

"Exactly right. You see, you and your mates built a float, hoping that the message would get through, no matter what the consequences, but you went through with it. And most important, you believed in it, and you went through with it."

"Is he still going to call for my friends' parents to come to the house and talk to them about what their sons did?"

"No, he isn't going to do that. But he is still sticking to what he believes."

"Then why am I here?"

"Your father and I had a meeting not too long ago. He called me in to consult with him on this problem concerning a dream that you had. Having you here will give us time to work alone with no interference."

"So, all of this was a way to get me over here to work this dream out?"

"Yes."

"Why didn't my father just ask me to come and stay with you and work this out?"

"I'm only guessing, because he never came out and gave me the answer. I asked him the same question. I believe that by getting you over here, and safe with me, you didn't have the time to tell your friends what was going on."

"So he thought that I would tell my friends about the dream and, by doing that, the whole town would have found out and everyone would have panicked."

"Something like that. But remember, that is only a guess. We won't know, because your father wouldn't tell me."

"Tell me, Stephen, what do you think of my dream?"

"I believe as your father does. It is of the utmost importance. We are going to have to do this together. It was your dream and you will have to tell me everything you remember."

"Why isn't my father involved with this? Why aren't the three of us working this out together?"

"Your father insists that he wants to work alone. He wants me working with you. So, actually, we are all working together, but in different houses. Do you understand?"

"I understand."

"So, if it's all right with you, I would like to start this meeting between you and me after you get a good night's sleep. We will start first thing tomorrow morning after breakfast. How does that sound?"

"Sounds fine. There is one thing that I would like to request," I said.

"What's that?"

"As I look around this office, I am noticing a lot of astronomical equipment. Not only that, I am noticing a lot of cauldrons and tons of jars filled with stuff. Over there in that far corner, you have a stack of books and, across the way, I see a large window. In front of the window is a telescope. In order to get to that telescope, you must walk up at least twenty steps. On the platform sits the largest telescope I have ever seen. It's your eyes to the stars, isn't it?"

"It's a passion of mine. Everything else you see around you are experiments that are not yet quite finished. I am always inventing new spells and using ancient spells to help me in my work. That's why those old books are opened. Research is very important to a witch. You are constantly learning and reading and researching, for the betterment of your kind. I say our kind, because anybody else has a hard time believing what we are doing, so we keep things to ourselves."

"Can I have a short tour before I go to bed?"

"It's still early. I can give you a short tour now. This way, we can get down to business first thing in the morning."

"Okay, then let's begin," I said eagerly. "It all looks so interesting."

CHAPTER 14

The sun had come up on a new day. Cousin Stephen and I were in the kitchen finishing up breakfast.

"Stephen, I wanted to thank you again for the tour last night and especially for this fine breakfast."

"Wasn't it good? It was cooked for us by Motam's wife, Gretta. She's the best cook I have."

"Stephen, there is a question that I wanted to ask you last night, but it slipped my mind."

"Ask away."

"I just wanted to know, how long do you remain the Witch of London?"

"Good question. It's actually a job for life, but I have the option to retire if I want to."

"How does one become the Witch of London?"

"Another good question. Once the position is vacant, a committee from London goes on a search for a new qualified witch. After many interviews and test taking, I was pronounced the new Witch of London."

"But, Stephen, you don't live in London."

"Don't have to. As long as I go to London when needed to take care of business, then I am fulfilling my obligation. And as you can see, it comes with a lot of privileges."

"What exactly are your duties?"

"Your father is head of the community. I am head of a committee of witches that take care of problems concerning London and a few of the surrounding towns. For example, last year, on the west side of London, two witches were having an argument. The bad thing was, they were both drunk and throwing spells around with their wands. They were both out of control. I was called in to stop them."

"Did you stop them?"

"I not only stopped them, but because they both continued and refused to stop what they were doing, I turned both of them into mules. Now they can be as stubborn as they want. But don't worry, the spell will only last for three months and then they will go back to being themselves."

"What else are you responsible for?"

"I am responsible for any unexplained events. An easy way of explaining what I do is to think of me as the head detective on a case. I am also the head scientist. One of my jobs is to try to cure unknown diseases."

"Wow. You do have a lot of responsibilities."

"I am also responsible for the upkeep of Stonehenge, which is right down the road. That's why I have the key to open the gates. I also run experiments at Stonehenge as well. I'll tell you more about that later."

"Now I know why you were given such a large house and also why you have the best equipment at your fingertips."

"That's right, and I will tell you more about my position some other time. I will tell you this. The government pays my bills here. That helps me out a lot. Right now, we have some business of our own to get to. We should not waste any more time."

"Okay. Let's begin," I said.

"All right, let's begin."

I looked at the mess in the kitchen. "What about these dishes? We just can't leave them on the table like this."

"Leave them, Cecil. I have a crew that comes in to clean up."

"Is there anything that you do on your own?"

"A few things. Especially my job. I work alone. Nobody works with me. This dream of yours is the exception. Now, let's get to my office so that we may begin." We went down the long hall to Stephen's office.

"Are you ready, Cecil?"

"Yes."

"Then let's begin. The best place to start would be from the beginning. Cecil, please, from the beginning."

"Okay. My name is Cecil Longstreet and I was born on…."

"Very funny. Can you please be serious?"

"Okay. When I was a young lad of five, my father told me that if you have a dream that brings you to tears, then that dream will most likely come true. Well, about a month ago, I had that kind of dream."

"Were you frightened?"

"Yes, very frightened."

"Please, tell me what made you cry?"

"The dream was very disturbing. There was a lot of destruction and an enormous number of lives lost."

"Cecil, what caused the destruction?"

"A meteorite."

"Where was this meteorite heading to?"

"It went straight for the south side of town. It was large enough to cover every square inch of the south side. After the impact of this massive meteorite, it exploded into a million pieces and left a hole in the ground. The hole was thousands of feet deep."

"You mentioned the destruction that occurred on the south side. Did anything happen to the north side?"

"That's the strange part of my dream. The meteor impacted just over the lake on the south side. It didn't hit the north side."

"Is there anything you want to tell me about this dream that I haven't asked you?"

"The dream felt so real. The sound of the impact was loud and the people-- the people were screaming and destruction was everywhere, but that too felt so real. I woke up crying. I then ran down the stairs towards the kitchen, screaming."

"You're shaking, Cecil. Relax."

"Am I?"

"Is there anything else you want to tell me?"

"Just that it was so real. Haven't you ever had a dream that seemed so real that you felt you weren't dreaming at all?"

"Sure."

"All of those people running and screaming. The worse part of all was the conclusion. The impact. After all was said and done, there was complete silence on the south side. Not a sound to be heard. You couldn't hear the beautiful sounds of the birds chirping, and not a dog was barking."

"What did the final scene look like?"

"I walked up to the lake, and all I saw was a wall created by the massive pieces of the meteorite. It must have been two miles high and was resting on the edge of the lake. Wait. There was a sound. The sound was coming from the lake. The fish were swimming in the lake, and every once in a while, a few fish would jump out of the water and land back into the lake. The splashing of the water was the only sound. It was all so sad. Now, on the north side, the flowers were in bloom, birds were singing their songs, dogs were frolicking about and barking. Children were playing, too, despite all of the destruction on the south side. At impact, the town of Stoneway was split into two different worlds. It was as if the people in the north didn't care about what had just happened to the people in the south. There was no concern at all for those poor people. You might as well ask me, how did I know that no one cared? Well, no one came over from the north to help out. Not one person."

"Why do you think that happened? You know, nobody caring?"

"One very good reason. My father told the community that if anyone crossed over the bridge, they would get locked up."

"And even when you are not dreaming, you have the same concerns for the welfare of the people in the south?"

"Yes, yes I do."

Stephen pointed to the gigantic telescope. "Let's take a look. What do you say?"

"Brilliant idea, Cousin."

"I know Cecil, I know."

So Stephen and I walked up the steps leading up to the telescope. I was watching his every move. He was hitting several buttons and turning a lot of dials.

"Cecil, please come over here. I have something for you to do."

"Yes?"

"Hold this lever still. We need this lever to hold the main part of the telescope in position. Let's see, I have a pad up here somewhere, yes, there it is. I always need my pad to calculate degrees and positions, etc., etc. Cecil, from what direction was the meteorite coming?"

"It came over us in the north and crashed down on the south side of the lake."

"So it came from the north?"

"Yes."

"Let's aim this baby into the heavens of the northern skies. Let's see what's going on up there. Cecil, one more important question. In your dream, what time of the day would you say it crashed in the south?"

"I believe it was late morning, but I am really not sure."

"Don't worry about that, I have another question. Where were you in the dream?"

"I was on top of a hill looking down towards the lake."

"Let me finish these calculations and then we can get started. It's important to have a starting point when you are looking for something. It's a large universe out there, and we are looking for an object that could be the size of a pin."

I waited patiently. I knew, and everyone else knew, that Stephen was the best in the business at what he does.

"We are ready to begin. Cecil, push that button, the red one to your left towards the bottom…there. Right."

I pushed that button. The telescope started to swing around ever so slowly. This motion continued until Stephen's coordinates were read completely by the telescope. After that happened, the telescope stopped turning.

"Okay Cecil, we will now begin to view the universe and the heavens above."

Stephen pointed to a lens on the telescope. He wanted me to look through it. Stephen had his own lens to look through. Now we could both view the sky at the same time.

"Cecil, you are seeing what I am seeing. Isn't this wonderful?"

"Stephen, this is amazing. Would you teach me more about the telescope when you have the time?"

"Sure."

"Cecil, you do realize that this is a long shot. The odds of our finding that meteor are not good. Just hope that luck is on our side."

"Stephen, I was wondering. Could this dream of mine be just what it is, a dream and no more? Are we making too much of this?"

"Let me ask you a question. You did cry because of this dream. Is this true?"

"Yes."

"Is your father, the mighty wizard taking this lightly?"

"No."

"Don't you think that if your father wasn't bothered by what you just told me, that he would be going through all of this? And besides, what if this is really true and we didn't try to do something?"

"So treat it as if it were something that could happen," said Cecil.

"Exactly. Now, let's look through this telescope and see what we can see."

"Look at that! Wow, did you see that, Stephen?"

"Of course I did. It was a shooting star. It is unusual to see one before sunset."

"I'm really liking this, Stephen."

"Cecil, do you feel like you are being punished, now?"

"Not in the least. I completely forgot that this was supposed to be a punishment. This is more of an educational experience."

"I never thought of it that way, but it does make sense," remarked Stephen.

An hour had gone by before Stephen came to a conclusion.

"Cecil, the skies are just too light right now to see anything of interest. I have an idea. We'd be better off waiting for nightfall. We will see much more then. It's actually my favorite time to stargaze. I'll be able to explain some beautiful sights to you."

"Sounds good to me, Stephen."

For the rest of the afternoon, Stephen showed me around the mansion. He also introduced me to a lot of gnomes. Some gnomes sleep during the day because they perform their duties through the night. So I would have to wait until later to be introduced to more of them.

While walking through the mansion, I found a room of interest. A yellow door caught my attention.

"Cousin Stephen, what's in that room?"

"Which room?"

"The only room on this floor with a door that is painted yellow."

"Oh, that one. That's my library and my study. Would you like to see it?"

"Yes, please."

We walked over to the door and Stephen opened the door and held it for me.

"You may enter."

I walked in and just stood in one spot, not moving a muscle. "This is incredible. I thought my father had a lot of books."

"There are exactly 225,337 books on these shelves. There are another 37 in my office. That makes a grand total of 225,374 books. And I am sure that somewhere around here, there are more books. I just don't get to all of the rooms. There are just so many of them."

"Do the gnomes borrow books from you?"

"There are only a few who are allowed to borrow my books, but they have to ask me first. They never take my books without asking."

"This room is twice the size of my father's office. Stephen, how old are some of these books?"

"Cecil, I'm going to show you the oldest book in my collection."

Stephen took his wand from the desk and pointed it towards the very top shelf.

"SE-AL-BUS CON-STRAY-GO."

As he said the words, the book walked itself off the shelf and once off the shelf, it floated down into Stephen's hands, which were wide open ready to receive this treasure. He turned to me.

"This book was written in 1603. It has 1,000 pages full of old spells. Now, as you know, spells do not lose their magic. Spells will always work, no matter how old they are."

"What is the title of this book?"

"It is called…ASTRONOMICAL SPELLS."

"Stephen, let me guess. If you have to change the direction or destroy a meteorite, this book might just have the spells."

"Are you sure you haven't read this book before?"

"Just a lucky guess," I said with a blush.

"We might need this book, Cecil. I will take this book back to my office and study it. Meanwhile, I am going to suggest that you spend some time in our game room on the main floor."

"Do you think that this book will work?"

"Cecil, just remember one thing while you are here. In my world, anything's possible. We will do our best to find and stop this meteorite."

"I hope so."

"Now, where was I…Oh, right. Step into the hallway and a gnome will escort you to the game room. I believe that you will totally enjoy it."

"Sounds good."

"I'll catch up to you later. It's almost time for supper anyway. I'll have someone come and get you from the game room when supper is ready."

"See you later," I said.

I opened the door and peeked into the hallway. I looked to the left and then to the right. The hallway appeared to be empty. I then took two steps, and found myself in the middle of the hall.

Suddenly, a small voice appeared out of nowhere. "Cecil Longstreet."

I turned around and found nobody, and then turned around again…no one in sight. Then I thought to look down by my right shoe. A gnome gave me a wave with his tiny hand.

"Always look down when you hear your name being called," said the gnome.

"Thanks for the advice. And when I saw no one around…I thought I was hearing voices."

"Someone is always around. You and anyone else who enter this house are constantly being watched. There is no escaping that."

"What's your name, little one?"

"My name is Gota. I am one of the sons of Motam."

"Come to think of it, you do look young, and no white beard. Tell me, do all gnomes wear white beards?"

"Only the men."

I smiled and then knelt down in front of Gota, extending my hand.

"Glad to meet you." We shook hands.

"Please take me to the game room."

"Follow me. That room is a hangout for the young ones, like myself. If you're lucky, you'll find a pinball machine to play with."

We started walking, Gota leading the way, and I following right behind him.

"Gota, how old are you?"

"I'm a baby. I'm 20 years old."

"I'm going to be 11 tomorrow, so I guess that makes me an infant if I were a gnome. How old is your father, Motam?"

"He's a young man. He's only 70 years old."

"How old is old to you?"

"I would say around 98 to 105 years old."

"Unbelievable."

I shook my head in disbelief as we made our way down the long hallway leading to the game room.

Later, I joined Stephen at the dining room table. This is no ordinary table. It's so long that it can seat 52 people. Stephen sat at one end and I sat at the other.

Gnomes were everywhere, several serving food. Some were picking up the dirty dishes, and others were filling up our glasses. There was a constant flow of gnomes. There were even gnomes replacing our dirty napkins.

At last, my plate was empty, and not a drop more could I eat.

"That was real good. Thank you."

"You're very welcome," said Stephen.

"Do you always eat dinner in this room?"

"Actually, no. This is a special occasion."

"What's the occasion?"

"You are my guest."

"Thanks."

"Anytime."

Stephen looked out the window and noticed it was getting dark.

"We should be getting back to my office. We have a telescope to look through."

CHAPTER 15

"All right, it's nice and dark outside and it's time to show you some great sights."

"Are we also going to look for the meteorite at the same time?"

"If we happen to see it. Anyway, the meteorite fell during the daytime. Cecil, I just remembered. I never asked you the most important question of all."

"What question would that be?"

"What day of the week did the meteorite crash?"

"Let me think." I took a while to think about the question.

"Do you remember?" asked Stephen.

Now I was getting frustrated. "I'm trying to remember."

I thought some more. "It was on a Thursday. That's it, a Thursday."

"Please, this is important. Tell me why you think it was on a Thursday?"

"Because the families were flying to market. And Thursday is Market Day."

"Who told you that those people were flying to the market?"

"A friend of mine came over to me and reminded me of why we had so much air traffic."

"You just made our job much easier. Today is Monday. So, that means that between today and Thursday, the meteor will be getting closer. We have a better chance of seeing it, the closer we come to Thursday."

"Cousin Stephen, something has been bothering me."

"What's bothering you?"

"Do we really know that this is the week that this will happen?"

"The best witch in the community told us so."

"I thought that no one in the community knew about this."

"May I remind you that the best witch in our community is your mother, our queen?"

"Well, that's different. You can be sure that this Thursday is the day," I said.

"Now that we got that all off of our chests, what do you say we look through the lens? You are about to receive your first lesson in stargazing. Hold on tight. You are about to get an education you will never forget."

And I believed what Stephen said. I knew that I was about to learn from the best there is.

CHAPTER 16

"Look into your lens," said Stephen.

"I haven't taken my eyes off it."

"Cecil, do you have any idea what you are looking at?"

"All I see is a bunch of stars."

"I am going to try to make this real simple for you. Those stars out there represent a symbol or a picture of some kind."

"I appreciate that."

"Let me zoom in a lot closer for you. Now, Cecil, I am going to ask you to use your imagination. Dead center in your lens is a group of stars. Can you visualize an object from those stars?"

"Give me a second."

"Here's a hint. It's the URSA MAJOR."

"You're kidding, right? What kind of a clue is that? All right, wait. It looks like some kind of pot…not a clue."

"It's the Big Dipper."

"I've heard of that one. So that is what it looks like. Fantastic!"

"Are you ready for another star puzzle?"

"Yes, I am ready."

"Let me position the telescope to this part of the sky. I'll turn that dial and push this button…here we are. Now I'll focus in and ask you if these stars look familiar. I'll give you a hint. It's between LYRA and CORONA BOREALIS."

"You're a funny guy, you are."

"Another hint. It's a man's name, and it starts with an H."

"My friend Henry has a star named after him."

"No. What you're looking at is Hercules. Again, I've put him right in the center of your lens so that you will know what I am talking about. Let's go to the next one."

"Cousin Stephen, you are really smart."

"Just keep reading and studying, and most important of all, pay attention to what your father says when you are talking about your studies."

"I do pay attention, but will my father even tell me where the stars are or what they look like?"

"Keep studying, you're still in the beginning stages. Keep listening, you'll find out."

"Stephen, let's go to another series of stars."

"All right, here we go, and here we are. Any idea what that star is?"

"It is bright. I am going to guess."

"Go ahead, guess."

"The North Star."

"Better know as URSA MINOR…the North Star."

"Yes! I got it right."

"Cecil, let's go back to the sky over our community."

"Good idea. That was fun. I really enjoyed that. Stephen,

when this is all over, can I come back here and learn the particulars, like how you get coordinates and degrees? I also want to know and learn how I can find planets."

"I can teach you, but I don't want to interfere with your studies. You can also come over and use the game room as long as your father allows you to."

"Thank you. This place is the best."

"The telescope is now set into position so that we have a view of the sky above us. Are you looking through the lens?"

"Yes, I am, but I have a question."

"What is it?"

"Stephen, look in the center of your lens."

"All right. Cecil, are you trying to tell me that what I am looking at is a meteor?"

"I'm the amateur. What do you think?"

"I can't rule it out. Let me put a fix on this so that we can track it."

Stephen began to do his magic. He turned knobs and pushed buttons.

"What exactly did you just do, Stephen?"

"Well, Cecil, I put this X on the object and now the telescope knows to follow it. It's one of the few telescopes in the world that can do that."

"You're making it sound very easy when I know it isn't."

"After putting the X on the object, you do have to know how to tell the telescope to follow it. There are only a few people who know how to operate this piece of machinery. Okay, it's all set. The meteorite is heading towards the direction of the south side. You also have to remember, that the line between the North and South is very thin. If the meteor goes off course one degree, it could destroy us."

"I would never have thought of that."

"Not only did I think of that, but your father thought of it first."

I just smiled.

"Cecil, it is getting late, and we have accomplished a lot for one evening, so why don't you retire for the night and I will stay here. I want to follow this meteor for a few more hours. Oh, by the way, good job."

"I actually found the meteor. Beginner's luck," I said.

CHAPTER 17

Today is my 11th birthday. What I didn't know until later was that I would be having some visitors coming over to the mansion to surprise me. I was never told what the gnomes had been cooking up, just for me, on my special day.

Stephen finally went to sleep about 4:00 in the morning. He was about to tell me what he had seen and what his thoughts were about the meteor. The breakfast dishes had been cleared away and all of the gnomes had left the area. Stephen felt that this was a good time to talk to me.

"Cecil, I had a very interesting evening--and morning, for that matter."

"When did you finally go to bed?"

"About 4:00 in the morning."

"Anything to tell me?"

"The telescope is doing its job. Performing beautifully. As per my calculations, there is a probability that Thursday is the day. All is going accordingly to your dream. It does crash on Thursday and, so far, everything is just like you saw it."

"Stephen, am I to be afraid of what I dream?"

"Cecil, you don't have a choice on what you dream about. There's one thing you must never do, and that is to ignore your dreams. And you may never hold back anything from us about what you dream. Especially if it has anything to do with destruction and the like."

As we talked, the front door bell rang. Dunkin answered the door and let the surprise guest in.

"Is anybody home?" shouted the wizard, who was accompanied by his queen.

Stephen let out a yell from the kitchen.

"We are back here, Uncle."

"Your aunt is with me as well."

"Welcome, my queen. You are always welcome here."

The wizard and the queen were escorted to the kitchen by Dunkin.

I got up from my chair. "Father, Mother, what a nice surprise."

"We didn't want you to think that we forgot your birthday."

"Okay, everyone just stay right here, and make yourself at home around the kitchen table. This will only take a minute," said Stephen.

Stephen left to get the cake from a refrigerator in another room. He returned holding the cake with 12 lighted candles on it. One extra for good luck. As soon as Stephen appeared, they all joined in on singing happy birthday to me.

"Happy birthday to you…." They all clapped and wished me a happy birthday with all good wishes.

"Son, I have a present for you. Would you want it now, or when you return home?"

"What do you think, Father?"

"Now."

"Right," I said and laughed.

The wizard reached into a pocket in his cape. He brought forth a small box, neatly wrapped with the family seal waxed onto the paper, to fully seal it.

"I have waited years to give you this present. I want you to know that I am proud of you, because you seem to have a gift that is so extraordinary, which leads me to believe that you are going to make a great witch, and maybe someday a wizard. I can tell by the way you are breezing through your books that you have what it takes. As you know, you have a long ways to go before you become a witch. I am very interested in your dreams. Having dreams that come true is truly a gift. It could be a scary gift, but at the same time, it can help us deal with anything that is thrown at us. Back to our gift to you. Your mother and I want you to have this."

My father, the wizard, handed the box to me and asked me to open it. I eagerly ripped off the paper and opened the three by five box.

"This is absolutely beautiful…what is it?"

"It's the family crest," answered his mother. "It's something that belonged to Winston Longstreet. It has been in the family for over 300 years," she continued.

I held in my hand a necklace of gold with a circular disk hanging from it. It wasn't any ordinary disk; it was a disk of magic.

"Wearing this will protect you from evil. You are not a witch yet, and you can't fend for yourself," said the wizard.

"I don't know what to say. This must be very valuable. I don't know if I can accept this. I mean, how can I wear this all of the time?"

"You can wear it all the time, because you are royalty. That means you can do whatever and wear whatever you like and when you like," said the Queen.

"May I put it on now?"

The wizard nodded, giving me approval. "Put it on."

I put it on and immediately felt somehow that I had worn this before.

"Son, it looks like you have been wearing this for a very long time," said my father.

"This disk isn't going to come off of the chain, is it?"

"No, it will never come off that chain," answered the wizard.

"I mean, I would be so afraid of losing it."

"Stop worrying, and just wear it," demanded my mother.

"Do I have to rub it and speak into it…."

"No, just wear it and it will protect you. It's as simple as that."

"How did this disc get so powerful?"

"Winston put a spell on it, and the spell will last forever… just as long as you are wearing it," said the wizard.

I traced the image on the disk with a finger.

"I can't think of a better birthday present...thank you, thank you all so much."

"You're very welcome, Son," said my parents in unison.

After everyone had enjoyed the birthday cake, Stephen made an announcement.

"Why don't we all go into the living room so I can fill you in on what's happening in the skies above," said Stephen.

"As you know, Cecil and I have been working with the telescope. You'll be glad to know that your son, Cecil, is going to make a very good astronomer some day. After searching the skies, your son found the meteor. That's right, he found it."

"It was just luck," I said, embarrassed at all the attention.

"Luck or no luck, you found it, Son," my mother said softly.

"It was like living his dream over again. Everything is happening just like he dreamt it. Not only that, the meteorite is heading for the south side. I also told him that if the meteor changes one degree, it could hit the north side."

"Stephen, let us see what you are talking about," said my father.

So we all got out of our comfortable chairs and walked into Stephen's office and over to the telescope.

"This telescope has been set and it understands that it has to follow the meteor. So once Cecil found it, the rest was easy."

"So the telescope won't take its eye off the meteor?" asked my mother.

"That's right. Even when we are sleeping, the telescope is keeping its eyes on the meteor."

My father was very impressed.

"Technology. This has got to be the best telescope in the world."

"The government made sure that I had the best one. Here, take a look. Come up here."

The queen, the wizard and I walked up the stairs to the platform. The wizard put his eye to one of the lenses. The

queen was told where the other lens was and she put her eye
to the other lens.

"There it is. My son found it," said my father.

"Yesterday the meteor was much smaller, which means
that it is getting closer to impact," said Stephen.

"And on what day did you, Cecil, say that the meteor will
crash?"

"On a Thursday."

The wizard stood up straight and faced Stephen.

"I have to talk to you about stopping this meteor. I believe
that this will be difficult, but we must put our heads together.
We cannot delay anymore. My queen, I will stay here at the
mansion tonight, and you, please, take care of business in
our community."

My mother went back to the house and the men, including
myself, talked throughout the evening and into the morning
hours about how this meteor could be stopped. The most
important thing that I wanted to talk about was the safety of

the people of the south side. How do we tell them that they are going to be squashed by a meteor? Would my father decide not to tell them at all? That was the big question. Would it matter if we told them at all? This was a decision for my father to make. I just hope he shows a bit of compassion towards those people.

CHAPTER 18

I went to bed around midnight because I couldn't keep my eyes open. That left Stephen and my father around the telescope, trying to figure out what their next move would be. Listening to those two talk is a real treat. Imagine, two experts in their field, and I am listening to them.

One of their conversations dealt with spells. That's when Stephen showed my father the book on astronomical spells. Both men were in agreement about what spells would be used to stop the meteor. In the meantime, I went to bed thinking about those people on the south side. Should they be told about the meteor? I also thought about the idea of telling them to get out of town. It would be a shame to lose everything that you own, but at least you would live another day. With these questions and thoughts in my mind, I drifted off to sleep. That is all that I remember.

The wizard was looking through one of the lenses of the telescope while Stephen was turning pages searching for helpful spells from several books. Stephen once told me that you couldn't have enough spells.

"Stephen, by the looks of that meteor, it is a big one."

"It sure is. And the closer it gets to earth, the larger it will appear. What a scary sight."

"I was thinking. There is a spell that will stop objects in midair and let them hang where they were stopped. They can't move until you say the second spell, and then they would continue on their way. The only problem with that spell is that you don't want it continuing."

"No, but if you could stop it, and then destroy it while it sits there like a chicken ready to be slaughtered, defenseless, then that is what we want," Stephen suggested.

"I see one problem. We really don't know the size of the objects that this spell can handle. It could probably stop a baseball in midair, but could it stop an object the size of this meteor?"

"I can see that more research is needed. At least, we have pinpointed a spell. Now we can work from there," said Stephen.

So back to the books went my father and Stephen. Only two more days to go and not a word about those poor people in the south. I must say something, and I must say it now before it is too late.

"Father, may I have a word with you?"

"Sure, Son, but finish your breakfast first."

Why did he brush me off like that? I just felt that my question was more important than breakfast. "But, Father, I must talk now before it is to late."

"Finish your breakfast first, then we shall talk."

I ate as fast as I could.

"Father, now may I ask you a question?"

"Yes, go ahead."

"Father, if the meteor is heading for the people in the south side, don't you think we should tell them what is going on? Don't you think we should give them enough time to gather their stuff up and move to another town? You have never mentioned anything concerning them. Do you dislike them so much that you are willing to let them get crushed by that meteorite?"

My father grabbed his chin as if he were in deep thought. Not answering me right away made me think that he really didn't care. I believed that I had gotten my answer.

"Do away with them completely, is that what you are thinking, Father?"

No response by my father. Complete silence, as if I weren't in the room at all.

I had never done this before, but I walked out of the room and went directly up to my bedroom. I was, of course, accompanied by a gnome. What really bothered me was that my father didn't even try to get me back to the room so that he could talk to me—to at least reprimand me...nothing.

Tomorrow is Wednesday and something has to be done! I walked back out of my room and headed downstairs to the kitchen where my cousin and my father were having breakfast. I walked into the kitchen and there was complete silence, as if I hadn't been missed or had said nothing wrong to upset anyone.

"Aren't you going to say anything to me, Father?"

"What's there to say?"

"I walked out on you."

"Should I get angry?"

"Yes, you should get angry! Half of our town is going to be wiped out and you, as our wizard, are not doing anything about this. Yes, you should get angry."

"What makes you so sure that I haven't already done something?"

I really didn't have an answer for that. The feeling that came shooting right through me was something I had never experienced. Was my father really going to do something?

"So, you're going to do something?"

"I didn't say I would, but maybe I already have?"

"Father, you're playing games with people's lives. Don't you see that? Now, are you doing something for those people?"

"Why don't you go outside or go to the game room for now?"

"Father, I will go to the south side and warn those people. Whatever the consequences to me!"

"Is my son raising his voice and threatening the wizard?"

I put my head down to my chest. Am I losing it? I had never raised my voice to my father. He's making me feel bad that I care.

"Father, are you going to save those people?"

He just looked into my eyes as if I should be expecting a spell to stop me from thinking like I cared.

"Son, why don't you join your mother at the house? Maybe she can use your help?"

"You're really not going to tell me, are you?"

"Have I answered you?" asked the wizard.

"Yes, I believe you have, Father."

CHAPTER 19

Today is Wednesday, and not a word about what my father will do for those people on the south side. This is so frustrating to me. I really meant it…I am this close to going over to the south side and warning these people. What will my father do to me? He will never make me a witch. Do I trade this off for saving the lives of those people? Why should a kid my age have such a dilemma put upon his head? This is not fair to me.

Lying here in bed has given me an opportunity to think. Sometimes thinking when you are not in a good mood is not good for you at all. I must get up and do what I have to do.

I went downstairs, only to meet a gnome in the hallway.

"What's your name?"

"My name is Rotem. What's your name?"

"I'm Cecil Longstreet."

"Motam's son told me about you. He would have walked you downstairs, but he was busy in the game room."

"Rotem, have you ever thought of leaving this house and starting your own life?"

"But this is our life. We know of no other."

"So, you really like it here?"

"We have everything here. Why would we leave?"

"You don't mind serving your witch?"

"We do as he says. He provides for us."

"But, you are really not free. I mean, you don't even go off the property."

"Why leave? Where would we go?"

I finally reached the kitchen, but nobody was there.

"Rotem, please take me to the Witch of London's office."

I followed behind and was escorted right to the door of the office. Rotem didn't leave me until I entered the room.

Being that the door was left open, it was easy to see that no one was in the office.

"Rotem, please escort me outside. Please lead the way."

Going out the front door, I realized that Rotem had left me. He was nowhere in sight. Straight ahead of me were two figures walking to a hill overlooking the north side. This hill also provided a view of the south side. Why would my father and Stephen be walking up that hill? Mind you, it wasn't a high hill, just high enough to be able to look down and observe what was going on around them.

I ran off the property and towards the hill. Were my cousin and my father going to go over to the South to warn the people? Running over to them, I was hoping to find out what they were up to. Would they actually tell me? I certainly planned to find out. Here I was running with a 300-year-old pendant around my neck, hitting my chest ever so hard.

"Father, please stop."

Stephen and my father turned around and looked at me with concern. You know, the look that says, "What are you doing here?"

"Father, are you headed towards the south side? That's all I want to know."

"Son, I think that it is time to tell you to turn around and join your mother at the house."

"Why are you ignoring me?"

"I will do what I have to do. It isn't any of your concern at the moment. Today is Wednesday, and that meteorite has to be stopped. Now, do you think I have time to stand here and argue with my 11-year-old son about the freedom of people who are living on the south side? For heavens sakes, I am trying to stop the meteorite from coming down and doing astronomical damage."

"I know why you're doing this."

"What are you talking about? I am doing this because that THING up there has to be stopped."

"No, that's not the answer. You are doing this in the hope that it doesn't land on us. If you knew for sure that it was going to smash the people in the south, you wouldn't do anything to stop it."

"Stop talking rubbish. And that's what you're doing."

"Father, don't stop the meteorite…let it fall."

"I believe in your dream."

"You believe in 99 percent of my dream. Otherwise, you wouldn't be going through all of this."

"You must be careful with dreams. As of now, it looks like you've got an extraordinary talent, but the only way it can be proved is to let it come to earth. I am not willing to take that chance. Yes, I will admit, everything is going as per your dream…."

"Father, if you can't take the chance on where this is going to land, why haven't you told the people of the south side about this? You have never given me an answer."

This time, I got a blank stare.

"Are you that confident that these spells are going to work. Is that it? These spells haven't been tested in a case like this. You don't really know if it will work."

"Every spell in these books has been proven to work."

"But not on something this large. You must tell those people. Father, I meant what I said. I will go over to the other side and warn them. Do you realize that tomorrow this meteorite is going to level all of that land? Father, I hope this has nothing to do with what happened over 300 years ago. Tell me that that isn't true."

"All of a sudden we want to be friends with these people who hung our witches?"

"These are not the people, Father. The oldest person on that side is in his early 90s. You can't blame them for the past; it's not fair. And now you are willing to kill all of them for what you feel is right. If that is the way you feel, then you are no better than the worst dictators that this world has seen. There is something that you have not thought of."

"What would that be?"

"If this gets out, and it will, the world will want answers."

"The rest of the world cannot do anything to me. I am the Wizard of Stoneway! I am too powerful for any man on this planet."

"Father, do you hear yourself? You are sounding like a commander of an army who feels that he is indestructible. Are you a dictator, Father?"

"No, I am not a dictator. I am just looking out for my people."

"You leave me no choice, Father."

"Cecil, as your cousin and the Witch of London, please do not do what is on your mind," said Stephen.

"Can you tell me as well, why I shouldn't, Stephen? Are you just like my father, or is it that you are afraid of him and that you feel you must go along with his way of thinking?"

"Your father is an intelligent man."

"I know that my father helped you become the Witch of London. You feel that you owe him this. Stephen, this is a mistake. What if these spells don't work?"

"Then the people of the South will be wiped off the face of this earth."

"And you're all right with that?"

"Your father believes...."

"He believes that this will work, because I know, and he won't admit this, but he knows, that it is going to land in the South, and you believe that as well. You believe everything my father says."

"Cecil, that is enough. I let you go on too long. Now go back while your cousin and I figure this whole thing out."

The wind was picking up and my father's cape was beginning to dance around because of it. The clouds were getting darker and you felt the horror in the air because of that which was going to take place the next day. It was coming--you could feel it.

I left my cousin and my father and I headed in the direction of the bridge that crosses over to the South. I walked at a brisk pace, not daring to look back.

I didn't even hear their voices pleading with me to come back. Is my father going to let me go through with this? I am wearing the crest of the family around my neck. I am protected from any danger or spells. Come to think of it, my father and cousin cannot stop me.

As I was getting closer to the bridge, I still didn't hear any voices trying to stop me. I was less than ten feet from the bridge and determined to cross it. A bolt of lightning hit the bridge, breaking it into a thousand pieces. Now, nobody could get over it. I turned around and my father was holding his wand in his hand. He had destroyed the bridge so that I couldn't cross.

I jumped into the water and swam across. He never tried to stop me, nor could he stop me. Debris from the bridge was everywhere. Swimming amongst the pieces of wood was not easy. Determination can work miracles if you let it. I suppose that I have the stubborn streak of my father and the compassion of my mother.

Once on the other side, I turned around to see where my father was. Neither my father nor Stephen was in sight. They could have flown off so fast that I couldn't see them.

Now I was on my own. What a scary thought.

CHAPTER 20

I walked up the road from the lake towards the center of town. I passed City Hall on my right and still no sign of life. There wasn't a person around. I continued on, and realized that someone had to see me coming. With these yellow pants on, how could you miss me? Was I scaring people? Just the thought that I was walking on this soil might be frightening people. I come in peace, but how can I tell them. How would they know why I am over here?

I looked to my right and saw the open field that was the meeting place for that historic moment when my father shook hands with these people. I often wondered why he really bothered doing that.

Suddenly, overhead, a brisk wind could be felt. A figure landed in front of me.

"Son."

"Yes, Mother. Are you here to stop me?"

"Son, please come home. Your father is beside himself. He can't believe the way you talked to him."

"Well, excuse me, but if you look around today, you can see the trees and houses, and guess what, Mother, tomorrow, it will all be gone. You have feelings Mother. You would not allow this to happen. Have you tried to talk to my father?"

"The truth is, he won't listen to me. He is stubborn in his ways."

"Mother, I have to warn these people. I must tell them to gather what belongings they can muster up and leave this town. Wait, I see some kids playing. Look, beyond City Hall, there is a park. Mother, I must continue to walk this road and spread the word. I have to."

My mother flew off. No goodbye and good luck. She just flew off. My mother might have compassion, but she is not a strong woman. That was obvious to me now.

There was no question about it, I was definitely on my own.

CHAPTER 21

I continued to walk this dirt road and eventually came upon some adults that were gathered in front of a building. Someone spotted me and they all turned around to look at the guy with yellow pants coming up the road

"Look who's coming towards us…it's the wizard's kid. Wonder what he wants?" shouted someone in the crowd.

"Maybe he wants to turn us into frogs, or teach us to fly," shouted another man. The crowd had a good laugh with that comment.

"Let's wait here until he comes over to us," shouted women in the crowd.

As I was getting closer to the crowd, I reminded myself that I was taking a big chance, being this brave. Don't forget, I have no powers. This charm around my neck doesn't protect me from a quick right to my jaw.

I finally reached the crowd and silence came upon everyone. I spoke to the crowd after I got their attention.

"You probably wondering what I am doing here. Well, I'm going to tell you."

Another voice yelled out. "Do you come over to reclaim the land? Don't you people have enough?"

I focused on the approximate area from which those questions came.

"Whoever asked those questions over there, the answer to your question is *no*. No, I have not come back to reclaim any land. I have come to you in peace and to also tell you of something of importance."

Another voice spoke up, but as this continued, I never saw the faces of those who spoke. "You're not here to help us. Your people hate our people. Your father blames us for what happened over 300 years ago. He is not a man who is what you would call very reasonable."

"I am here to tell you that I don't blame you for what happened over 300 years ago. Please believe me when I tell you that I want to help you."

A man in the crowd wanted to know why I wanted to help them…all of a sudden.

"I want to help you, because you are all in danger."

A shout from the back of the crowd. "How are we in danger? Are you warning us of an attack from your father?"

"No, it's not like that. Here's what happening. A meteorite is headed this way and it will destroy every human being and animal south of the lake."

The people in the crowd were now talking to each other. This went on until I spoke up again.

"This is very serious!"

A man in the crowd yelled out. "Why are you trying to scare us? What will you gain from this prank?"

"This is not a prank, nor some kind of joke. I am here to tell you that you must leave this town, and you must leave now, for tomorrow the meteorite will crash down upon you, that is, if my father and the Witch Of London can't stop it."

A woman from the crowd called out. "This smells of something to get us out of this town, once and for all. Once we leave, your people will take this town over and we are out of a place to live."

"No, I assure you, that isn't the case. Please believe me when I tell you that I didn't have to come over to the South to tell you this. As a matter of fact, my mother and father are not happy at all that I disobeyed them in doing so. Maybe they can stop the meteorite…and then again, maybe they can't. This has never been done before, and we can only hope that my father and cousin know what they are doing."

"So you are serious about all of this?" called out a person from the crowd.

"Yes, yes I am. This meteorite is coming down on you tomorrow and you must leave. The best thing that can come out of this is that it can be stopped, and then you can come back and lead normal lives. What do you have to lose by listening to me? Just leave, and hope that all can return the next day, safe and sound. If the meteorite can't be stopped, then you can return…alive."

An elderly man from the crowd, which must have numbered in the hundreds, stepped out and walked towards me.

"Young man, you have a kind face, and you seem sincere about what you say. But let me ask you a question. Why are you doing this for us? Aren't we supposed to be your enemy, the people who hung your people, and all of that?"

"Listen, I know that the blame shouldn't be put upon all of you. I came to warn you, because lives are at stake here. There is no time for this foolishness, or who is right and who is wrong. I will not and cannot allow this slaughter to happen. Like I said before, let's hope that this meteorite can be stopped."

The old man looked at Cecil again.

"What is your name, young man?"

"I am Cecil Longstreet. The son of the Wizard and the Queen of Stoneway."

"I remember when you were born. You have grown up quite fast for a young man. I believe you when you say you want to help."

The crowd seemed to agree with the elderly man.

"We will pack what we can carry and be on our way. One more thing," said the old man.

"What's that?"

"Thank you, Cecil Longstreet," said the old man.

The crowd dispersed. They were all on their way back to their houses to pack what they could carry.

I felt good about what I did. I have no regrets. Going home is something that I do not fear now. The people are leaving and I can't imagine what my parents will do to me as a result of disobeying them. Hopefully nothing.

In a matter of an hour, the southern part of the town was deserted. Not a soul to be seen. I stood and watched the exodus for that hour, and I felt good about the possibility of having saved all of those lives.

It was now time to turn around and go back to my cousin's place.

CHAPTER 22

"Cecil, as your cousin, I have to tell you, that was a very brave thing to do. Going against your parents, especially your parents, was insane."

"Stephen, I had to do it. I couldn't let all of those people perish from the face of the earth because my father is too stubborn. Didn't make sense to me."

"Well, between you and me, it was the right thing to do. If you ever tell your parents what I said, I'll deny I ever said it."

"No problem. It's nice to know you're not afraid of my parents."

I gave Stephen a little smile. He smiled back and gave the thumbs up sign, which I returned.

"Where is my father, Stephen?"

"He went back to your house. He said that he would not return until tomorrow morning. At that time, he said that he would stand on top of that hill."

Stephen pointed to the hill overlooking the southern part of Stoneway.

"I was told to meet him there at 9:00 in the morning. I was also told to bring the book of spells and my wand. Oh, right, he wants you there as well."

"Why 9:00?"

"It has been calculated that, at that time, the meteorite can be seen with the naked eye. From 9:00, the countdown for the meteorite to crash will be at 10:00. We will have an hour to stop it from crashing."

"Stephen, can we really stop the meteorite?"

"We are going to have to believe that we can. You see that pendant around your neck? I was also told that it would be used when the meteorite comes into view. I understand that

that pendant has been involved with thousands of spells. It is the most powerful symbol that our people have still in existence. Remember, the more spells your wand performs, the more it gains strength. The same goes for that pendant. Powerful stuff, Cecil."

"So, 9:00 it is. I will be there. Pendant and all."

I walked away from Stephen and headed to my room. Oh, right, my friend escorted me back to my room. I don't believe that anyone could roam these hallways alone if they wanted to. These gnomes know their jobs. You don't have a chance to walk alone. But one thing that I can't understand… why aren't you allowed to walk alone? Pretty strange if you ask me.

The next morning came upon me quickly. Walking out of the house and heading towards the hill seemed like a dream to me. I couldn't believe what was ahead of us.

There they are. My father and cousin, in full costume, equipped with their books and wands. But why did they need me? The only thing I could figure out was that they needed my pendant.

"Good morning, Cecil," said Stephen.

"Good morning, Stephen," I answered. Then I looked at my father.

"Father, morning."

"Morning, Son."

"So, what's the plan?" I asked.

My father walked up to me and explained what my role was. I was right. It had to do with the pendant.

"Father, please, tell me the truth. Are you doing this to protect the people in the South, or are you doing this just in case that meteorite changes one degree, and heads for us?"

"I am protecting our people and that is all I am going to say. We have no time for this now."

I looked at him with that look of disappointment. He didn't seem to care how I looked at him. I have never seen him this serious, although this is probably the most serious situation anyone has ever been in. We now had a job to do, and I was part of it.

"Cecil, I want you to stand next to me. Never leave my side," demanded my father.

"Sir, what would you like me to do?" asked Stephen.

"Stephen, I want you to hold this book open to the page we discussed. When I give you the signal, put the book down and take your wand out. There's one important thing that you must not forget. Wherever I aim my wand, you aim your wand in the same direction. You copy my every move. We are going to need all of the power that we can put out. Two wands are better than one. This is going to drain everything out of us, so just be aware of that. Here, Cecil, you see that jar of water on the ground?"

"Yes."

"If by chance your cousin and I fall to the ground, have the water ready for us."

"It is now 9:15 and still nothing to look at. Wait, I see a speck in the sky," I shouted.

I pointed into the sky, in the direction of the speck. Both my cousin and father immediately looked in that direction.

"That's it, and I do believe it's early. Let's get started. Stephen, hold that book up to me, chest high."

The wind was starting to pick up. The trees were swaying and leaves and everything else flew through the air. This wind came on very fast. It was a scary feeling. There it was, now we had to stop it. But where will it crash, if we can't stop it?

"Cecil, stand right beside me. Now, take that pendant off of you and hand it to me."

So I handed the pendant to my father. The wind was so strong that it almost flew out of my hand. My father took the pendant and set it on the page, and then proceeded to speak the spells from this old, old, book.

"SEE-TUMBLY-SEE-GROTTA. TA-HALEY, SEE-GROTTA."

My father raised his hands as Stephen held the book and pendant at the same time. His cape was blowing in the wind with such force, my father had to move his right foot to the back, to brace himself from falling backwards. My cousin had the hard part. He had to hold the book and pendant at the same time.

"Stephen, put the book down...no, hand it to Cecil. Hold up the pendant and take out your wand. Do as I tell you. Aim it, Stephen."

As both of them aimed their wands, my father repeated the spell.

"SEE-TUMBLY-SEE GROTTA. TA HALEY, SEE-GROTTA!"

The meteorite now was moving with what seemed to be great speed. It was supposed to slow down once in the earth's atmosphere. It wasn't slowing down. This was not working.

"Father, it's coming this way! Father, do something!"

I was panicking, and I had every right to.

"Cecil, calm down," said Stephen.

"Calm down!"

"Stephen, aim the pendant at the meteorite."

The wind was now howling, as I fell back onto the ground. I was now on all fours. Oh, how I wish I had their powers.

"It's still coming at us. It is definitely heading towards the south side. Uncle, is there anything else we can do?" asked Stephen.

"We can only repeat the spell. We just don't know how many times it will take to stop it!"

As the spell was repeated several more times, the meteorite continued its journey. Its path was as they expected. It was overhead and that's when the strangest thing happened. It started to back up. That's right, it was backing up. It headed back up to the northern skies. Once it was almost out of sight, it exploded into a million pieces and a glow of light came from afar. It felt hotter than the sun. The sound was deafening to my ears. I found myself flat on my back again. The wind had stopped blowing. It had turned into a calm day. We ran towards the largest tree to shield ourselves from the falling pieces of meteorite.

"We did it! We did it!" shouted my father. He was actually smiling from ear to ear. He grabbed me and threw his two large arms around me.

"Son, we did it," he shouted as he looked into my eyes. "We destroyed the meteorite."

"Stephen, I don't know if I could have done this without you. Thank you for all of your help."

"It's called teamwork. I was glad to participate," said Stephen.

"And you, my son, thank you."

"What did I do?"

"You gave me your pendant to stop the meteorite. Before I forget, here it is."

My father put the pendant around my neck. He straightened it out, so that it was perfectly in the middle of my chest.

After the shower of meteorite pieces stopped, I noticed that our community came out to see the aftermath. Everyone was picking up a piece of the meteorite.

The next thing we knew, my mother was by our side and the community was surrounding the tree.

There was dancing and people were chanting. It was a party.

"Father, what about the people from the South?"

"Look over the lake, my son."

The people from the South were seen coming towards the lake…and that is where they stopped.

"Father, can those people cross over the lake?"

There wasn't an answer. My father put his head down as if he were thinking. It took a while, but his answer finally came.

"Son, let our neighbors from the South enter the North!"

I ran as fast as my little legs would carry me, but I soon realized that there no longer was a bridge. I looked back at my father and pointed to where the bridge once was. He understood what I was trying to tell him.

Pieces of wood started flying all over the place, as if he was running a movie backwards. The bridge was put back together, piece by piece. Once the bridge was put together, I ran over to the other side. I told the people to come on over…no strings attached. They believed me.

In single file, they all walked over the bridge and walked straight towards the tree just beyond the hill where my parents stood. I led them towards that tree. I was first in line for this historic moment.

We all stopped in front of my father, and waited for his words of wisdom.

"We are here, Father."

I didn't realize it, but the man behind me stepped out of line and walked up to my father.

"I extend my hand to you, my old friend."

My father shook his hand and suddenly I realized what he had just said: "old friend." Now I was puzzled.

"Mr. Mayor, there comes a time when even with all of my knowledge and power, someone comes along with far less knowledge and power and then teaches me a lesson. That someone would be my son."

Now everyone was looking at me. I looked back at my father and mother, two proud parents. What else could a kid ask for?

I walked up to my father and asked him a question. "Father, why did the Mayor call you an old friend?"

"Very simple. He is an old friend."

"And that is why you made the trip over the bridge?"

"Yes, that is why. That was the least I could do for him."

"But why?"

"Many years ago, before you were born, my friend here saved the life of a family member. I never forgot that. Now, I do believe we can live in harmony and peace. My friend, we shall sit down and discuss the particulars, so that we can remain a whole town."

My father cleared his throat and looked around. "I want everyone to hear this…the first act of kindness and togetherness will be to take the bridge down and fill in the lake. There is to be no more separation between the North and the South."

The crowd went wild. The dancing continued along with shouts of joy.

"We shall be real neighbors and mingle among each other."

Well, I guess I accomplished a few things. I realized my new power. I can dream, dreams that come true. It's still a scary thought. Hope I can dream good things as well. It took a meteorite to straighten my father out. I suppose one has to move mountains to get to the other side. Would have been easier to walk around the mountain.

And my dream of peace. That has certainly come true. I have more friends now, more than I ever could have imagined.

I am continuing with my studies. Someday I will reach my goal. And maybe, someday, I will be as wise as my father.

CPSIA information can be obtained
at www.ICGtesting.com
Printed in the USA
FFOW03n1106090414
4787FF